Sinbad
Legend Of The Seven Seas™

Junior Novelization

by **Eleanor Fremont**

DreamWorks®

PUFFIN BOOKS
Published by Penguin Group
Penguin Young Readers Group,
345 Hudson Street, New York, New York 10014, U.S.A.
Penguin Books Ltd, 80 Strand, London WC2R ORL, England
Penguin Books Australia Ltd, 250 Camberwell Road, Camberwell, Victoria 3124, Australia
Penguin Books Canada Ltd, 10 Alcorn Avenue, Toronto, Ontario, Canada M4V 3B2
Penguin Books (N.Z.) Ltd, 182-190 Wairau Road, Auckland 10, New Zealand

Published by Puffin Books, a division of Penguin Young Readers Group, 2003

1 3 5 7 9 10 8 6 4 2

Sinbad: Legend of the Seven Seas TM & © 2003 DreamWorks L.L.C.
Text by Eleanor Fremont

Puffin Books ISBN 0-14-250104-2

Printed in the United States of America

CHAPTER ONE

Long, long ago, in the mists of a time long past remembering, a story began. It started with a voice—a whisper that reverberated across the night sky, echoing among the twinkling stars, the swirling constellations, and celestial bodies. A soft, caressing whisper, it carried a hint of unimaginable danger.

After the voice came the form, gathering itself from within a fiery nebula, flowing effortlessly outward until it had taken the shape of a gigantic female.

This was Eris, Goddess of Chaos and Strife. She was devastatingly, bewitchingly beautiful. The tendrils of her long black hair floated for miles around her, and her midnight-blue gown spread out around her feet and swirled out among the galaxies. She strode confidently toward the tiny blue-and-white ball of Earth.

"Wake up, my beauties," she said in a caressing voice. "Rise and shine. It's a brand-new day and the mortal world is at peace. But not for long."

Gradually, organizing themselves from the billions of stars, the animals of the constellations flickered to life and gathered around Eris like her own ghastly cosmic menagerie. There were creatures real and imaginary: a crab, a firebird, a scorpion, a unicorn, a centaur, a sea monster. They glowed in pale, eerie colors, lit from within by the stars that formed them.

"Just look at them!" she said, peering down delightedly at the unsuspecting little planet. "I pull one tiny thread and their whole world unravels into chaos. Glorious chaos." She paused, noticing something: tiny ships speeding across a tiny blue sea. "And what could be more perfect than this," she continued. "A noble prince, a priceless treasure . . . and a blackhearted thief. Oh, this is going to be fun."

The constellation monsters snickered and scratched with glee. Lovingly, Eris took one of them, a dreadful-looking sea monster called Cetus, into her arms. It shrank back reluctantly, but there was no escape. She had made her choice.

"Cetus," she said. "You know what to do!" Then, with a flourish, she dropped the sea monster toward the ocean below on Earth.

"Let the games begin!" she cried.

No one on the deck of the *Chimera* saw Eris's sea monster splash into the ocean. They were too busy with their work: being pirates. The *Chimera*, small, light, and quick, was on the chase—just a boat-length behind an enormous royal flagship, and closing in fast. The *Chimera*'s Asian-style sails, shaped like fans, gave the ship the advantage of speed.

The pirate leader was pacing up and down on the deck of the *Chimera* before his very diverse group of roguish sailors. He was a rakishly handsome fellow with dark, flashing eyes, and he wore a turban. At his feet was a huge, jowly, slobbery brown dog. "Gentlemen," he announced, "this is the score we've been waiting for. The world's most valuable object is on its way to Syracuse." Then he broke into a mischievous grin of anticipation, the grin that identified him as the one and only Sinbad. "Shame it'll never get there," he added.

There was laughter from the crew, and a joyous bark from Spike the dog, as the *Chimera* drew up closer to the larger craft. The big ship's soldiers had by now gathered defensively along the rail, bracing for what was to come.

"After today," Sinbad told his men, "we retire to Fiji."

The men burst into cheers. Jin and Li, the twin Chinese pitmen, jubilantly chest-bumped each other. Muscular and athletic, they clearly relished a good fight. They were joined by Jed, the ship's weapons master, who brandished a fearsome-looking gun that could shoot dozens of arrows from its rotating barrel. And hanging upside down, as intense and eager as the rest, was Rat, the Italian rigger. Incredibly agile, Rat was constantly clambering around the rigging, always in motion.

Sinbad strode to the front of the ship, his men still cheering. "Kale!" he shouted.

"Aye!" came the response from the huge, bald man who was the first mate of the *Chimera*. His bald head and two earrings glinted in the sun as he stood on the topdeck, manning the wheel.

"Spike!" Sinbad called.

"Woof!"

Sinbad climbed the mast and surveyed his crew. "Let's get rich!" he yelled.

At his command, huge blades suddenly sprang out from the hull of the *Chimera*. It veered hard toward the huge flagship. With an explosive collision, the *Chimera* ground its blades into the hull of the larger vessel, anchoring itself firmly to its prey.

Then, from the *Chimera*, the men began to leap across to the deck of the big flagship as its armed soldiers rushed to its defense. The battle was on. Sinbad was the first across, leaping confidently into the fray. He was followed closely by Jin and Li. The brothers worked together as a team. Fighting acrobatically, they used their feet and a staff held between them as their only weapons. They threw vicious kicks to fight the flagship's defenders.

Now the tremendous Kale leaped onto the flagship. He was built like a mountain. Tearing a railing free, he used it to bat the soldiers aside. Jed, the weapons master, jumped across and produced a bunch of dangerous-looking swords with multiple blades. He ran off to join the battle. Above the fighting, the nimble Rat swung easily among the ropes, a knife held in his teeth. He swooped down and, using the curved blade of his scimitar, began disarming soldiers.

Then the flagship's soldiers started flying off the deck, knocked aside by something that moved through the crowd with great force. It was Spike, bounding across the deck, spewing gobs of slobber as he went. To the untrained eye, the big, goofy, fun-loving hound looked terrifying.

In the thick of the battle, Sinbad squared off against five or six soldiers, the last unified front of the scattered resistance. He flipped the helmet off one of the guards, revealing his matted hair. Sinbad head-butted the guard, knocking him out, whereupon the other soldiers rushed Sinbad with great energy.

"What are they feeding these guys?" Sinbad muttered. Oh, well, nothing to be done. In a dizzying display of martial arts culminating in a 360-degree circular sidekick attack, Sinbad defeated them all.

He sheathed his twin sabers as Kale approached, his end of the battle secure.

"Catch that last move? Pretty cool, huh?" said Sinbad.

Casually, Kale knocked the helmet off an attacking guard, using the heads of two of the others. "I thought you overworked it, just a bit," he commented to Sinbad.

Sinbad was flummoxed. "I—uh—you . . . Overworked it?!"

He was interrupted by a yell as one of the flagship's remaining guards swung his saber toward Kale's neck. Kale offhandedly caught the guard's massive blade in his teeth. Then, with a mighty flick of his neck, Kale sent the terrified guard, still holding the saber, flying over the side of the ship.

"Oh, and *I* was overworking it," said Sinbad disgustedly.

The two of them were distracted by a shout from up on the aft deck, where it seemed a sword battle was still raging. The last valiant soldier standing was single-handedly holding off three of Sinbad's men.

When they saw who it was, Sinbad and Kale exchanged a look of surprise. This was not just any soldier. This was someone they never expected to find here.

"Proteus," said Sinbad softly.

CHAPTER TWO

W ell," Kale said under his breath, "this just got interesting. How long's it been?"

"About a lifetime," Sinbad said quietly.

Proteus was fighting hard to keep Sinbad's men, Hassan, Luca, and Grum, away from the door leading to the cabins.

"You still fight like an old lady," Sinbad called to him.

"Sinbad?" Proteus turned, astonished—forgetting the fight for the briefest instant. In a flash, he was wrestled to the ground by Sinbad's men. Sinbad stepped past him with a smile, heading for the cabin door.

Proteus pushed himself to his feet, shrugging off Sinbad's men. "Sinbad! Wha-what are *you* doing here?"

"I'm working. You?" Sinbad jammed his dagger violently into the door lock, gave it a sharp twist, and yanked out the entire lock mechanism.

"Wait, wait, wait," said Proteus. "What happened to you? Where have you been?"

"I would love to stop and catch up," Sinbad said, "but I've got things to do, places to go, and stuff to steal." Opening the door, he strode into the cabin.

As Proteus followed Sinbad into the room, Kale stood aside and smiled.

Sinbad stopped, his eyes widening at what he saw in the cabin. "Ooooh . . . yeah," he said, with a low, reverent whistle.

Proteus quickly came up from behind him and put a hand on his shoulder. "Sinbad," he said. "We need to talk."

Sinbad simply smiled, pulled Proteus's hand off his shoulder, and pushed past him. "I've heard about it," he said, more to himself than to Proteus. "Read about it. But never actually seen it."

In the cabin, a large, ancient-looking book lay open on a central pedestal. On its pages were wondrous, mystical signs and symbols. A magical light glowed above it.

Sinbad was genuinely awed. As Proteus walked up beside him, Sinbad sighed. "The Book of Peace," he whispered. Everyone knew what the Book of Peace was. A gift of the gods, it was the most precious object in the Twelve Cities. It changed hands every one hundred years, and now it was returning to Syracuse. Without the Book, the cities would all fall to ruin.

"It's my job to bring it safely to Syracuse," Proteus told Sinbad.

The moment was broken. "Really? Well, see, now I feel bad, because—you're gonna get fired," said Sinbad.

"You can't be serious," Proteus returned. "You disappear for ten years. You show up and you *rob* me?"

"I wish it wasn't you. I do, really. But—"

"But it is me, Sinbad."

"Proteus, we had a special handshake, some code words, and our own neat little hideout," said Sinbad. "It was nice, but we were kids."

"We were *friends*. You're not going to steal this. Not from me. And what would you do with it anyway? The Book of Peace protects all of us in the Twelve Cities."

"Exactly," Sinbad replied. "So just imagine how much 'all of us' will pay to get it back."

"Sinbad, let me say it again. A long time ago, you and I were friends. If that ever meant anything to you, prove it now."

Sinbad stopped a moment. Then he shrugged and headed toward the Book. "You're right," he said. "That was a long time ago."

Proteus stepped in front of Sinbad. "If you want the Book," he said grimly, "you have to go through me."

"Now don't get all heroic, Proteus," Sinbad warned. He moved his sword slightly and Proteus immediately parried with his own. The sound of clanging steel rang through the room as they exchanged a flurry of blows. Their swords locked, and the two men glared at each other over the crossed blades. Deadly intent flared in the eyes of both.

And then—the room tilted. Both men spilled to the ground as the ship groaned and shuddered. Something big had hit the ship.

"What the—?" said Sinbad as he struggled to his feet. He and Proteus raced outside onto the deck.

"Dear gods," gasped Proteus as they both looked up to see a set of huge tentacles writhing over the deck, clinging and grasping blindly, pulling the ship down at the bow.

"Whooo, that is ugly!" Sinbad exclaimed.

Meanwhile, Sinbad's boat, the *Chimera*, had disengaged and begun to drift free of the flagship. Sinbad sheathed his sword. "Well, I see you're busy," he said hurriedly to Proteus. "So—I'll stay in touch!" No way was he staying on Proteus's ship.

"Wait! Wait!" Proteus cried. "You're just going to run away?"

Sinbad looked back briefly. "Uh . . . yeah," he said over his shoulder as he leaped down the stairs and sprinted for his boat.

He was almost knocked to his feet as one of the huge tentacles rocked the boat again. Then it reared up and crashed down onto the *Chimera*, smashing one of its masts.

"Sinbad!" Kale yelled helplessly.

The expression on Sinbad's face went from disbelief to anger. "You—my—my *ship*!" he spluttered at the tentacle.

As if in answer, the bow of the flagship gave a sickening lurch, and an enormous, terrifying sea monster heaved itself from the water. It was Cetus, cast down from the stars and in an earthly form. The monster's fanlike collar and scaly body made it a horrible sight. It looked a little like a giant squid on steroids.

Proteus and his men were attacking the sea monster as best they could. Dodging the flying tentacles, Proteus threw a spear. When that had no effect, he picked up a sword discarded by one of his fleeing men and charged again, stabbing a tentacle.

"Heads up," yelled a familiar voice behind him.

"Sinbad?" said Proteus, surprised.

Sinbad, standing atop a pile of barrels of gunpowder, was in the midst of lighting a fuse that went directly into one of the barrels. When he was done, he sprang down onto a board that was wedged between the barrels. This sent the barrel, burning fuse and all, flying through the air, straight toward the gaping mouth of the sea monster. Its pronged tongue grabbed the barrel.

It swallowed.

Sinbad walked over to Proteus, who had been knocked over by the monster, and helped him to his feet. "Now," he said, "stand by for sushi."

The barrel exploded. The monster belched and then

roared at them, showering them with sea-monster slime. The barrel had not agreed with it.

Proteus looked at Sinbad. The monster burped again and a swallowed guard was spewed back out onto the deck. The guard wiped the slime off his face, looked around, and charged right back into the battle.

"Give that guy a raise," Sinbad told Proteus, impressed by the guard's daring.

Proteus nodded in agreement. "Done," he said.

But they had relaxed too soon, for with a terrific undulation, the monster heaved itself farther onto the flagship, tossing Proteus's crewmen across the deck as it went. Proteus grabbed Sinbad's shoulder and started to pull him away.

As Sinbad turned, he noticed that a sword was stuck high in the mainmast. This gave him an idea.

"Come on, Sinbad, let's go," Proteus urged.

Sinbad stopped him. "Wait," he said. "Stand your ground." He turned to face the monster, a determined look in his eyes.

"What are you doing?" Proteus shouted.

Sinbad put two fingers into his mouth and whistled loudly. "Hey hey! Lobster boy! Over here!" he shouted, waving madly at the monster.

This got the beast good and irritated. It opened its mouth and shot out its enormous tongue, right toward them. At the last moment, Sinbad shoved Proteus aside, drew his sword, and—*whack!*—spiked the tongue to the deck.

As the monster struggled, its tentacles swiped dangerously across the deck. Sinbad rolled, dodging a tentacle, and landed near Proteus.

"Next time—tell me the plan!" Proteus yelled to him.

They both looked up and froze momentarily as the creature loomed above them.

"Okay," Sinbad shouted. "Run!" Proteus wanted the plan, Proteus got the plan.

They turned and ran. "Fall back!" Proteus shouted frantically to his men.

Behind them, the horrible creature rose up higher and lunged forward. Sinbad looked over his shoulder at the monster as they flew across the deck, and then scooped up a length of rope as he went.

"Grab hold," he said to Proteus as he lashed it around the mast. Proteus grabbed the other end of the rope.

Each man grasped the other's wrist.

"Let's go," said Sinbad.

Using their weight against the rope, holding each other's wrist, they climbed quickly up the mast. A tentacle wriggled up the mast behind them, but they managed to avoid it and pull themselves up onto the yardarm, the long, sideways boom that held up the sail.

Sinbad pulled the sword from the mast, and put it between his teeth. "C'mon!" he shouted.

"And the plan?" Proteus inquired.

"How about, try not to get killed," said Sinbad.

Proteus looked down. The sea monster covered the deck, and was wrapping its many tentacles around the mast.

Sinbad smiled and pulled the sword out of the mast. "Hold on!" he said, slicing through a rope and freeing one end of the yardarm.

They both held on to the ropes for dear life, Sinbad with his feet braced against the mast and Proteus with a tenuous foothold on the dangling yardarm. "Here," said Sinbad, tossing Proteus the sword, "you'll need this!"

"Where are *you* going?" Proteus asked as he caught the sword.

"Fishing!"

Sinbad scrambled to the top of the mast, pulled himself onto the rope that was stretched between the masts, and began to walk across like a tightrope walker in a circus. "Left, right, left, right," he muttered to himself, trying to keep from looking down.

The sea monster reared back and slapped a tentacle at him, wrapping it around his tightrope. Sinbad fell, but lunged and caught the rope, swinging over to land on the next yardarm. He pulled out his dagger. "Now!" he yelled, waving to Proteus.

Together, they cut the ropes supporting their yard-arms, sending them plunging toward the deck far below, with both men still standing on them. As they hurtled toward the huge head of the beast, Proteus and Sinbad both leaped off the yardarms.

"Woo hoo!" Proteus whooped.

"Wahoo . . . hoo . . . hoo!" Sinbad yelled with him.

The long yardarms stabbed into the sea monster, impaling it, and Cetus crashed to the deck, unmoving.

Sinbad and Proteus shared a big bear hug. "You okay?" asked Sinbad.

"Yeah, thanks for sticking around," Proteus replied.

They laughed as the monster slid back down into the deep, not noticing the last of its long tentacles slipping across the deck behind them. But suddenly the huge tentacle whipped across the deck toward them.

"Look out!" Sinbad cried. He shoved Proteus aside and caught the full weight of the thing himself. Reflexively, it coiled around him, dragging him off the ship and into the air.

"Sinbad!" Proteus shouted.

With a splash, Sinbad was dragged beneath the waves as Proteus dashed helplessly to the rail. His men could barely restrain him from going after his friend.

He looked down at the surface of the water. Sinbad had disappeared into the inky depths.

CHAPTER THREE

Cetus sank into the sea, dragging Sinbad down with him. Sinbad gasped for air, struggling against the death grip of the tentacle. He felt himself drowning.

Then, a strange, murky shape came swooshing through the water toward the sinking monster. Sinbad opened his eyes and looked again in disbelief as a huge face appeared before him. Of course, it was Eris, the beautiful and treacherous, her jet-black hair and her long gown billowing around her in the ocean. She blew a giant air bubble that surrounded Sinbad.

The tentacle released him. Gasping for air, he looked up to find himself on the dry ocean floor, surrounded by the enormous bubble in the water. He slowly struggled to his feet, looking around in amazement. All he could hear was a mournful voice.

"The day began with such promise," it said. "And now look. My sea monster is defeated and I still don't have the Book of Peace." Now Eris appeared inside the bubble, and her tone went from mournful to irritated. "All because of you, Sinbad," she said.

"You know who I am?" Sinbad asked.

"Oh yes. I've been watching for some time now," hissed Eris.

"Uh-huh," he said. "And you are. . . ?"

"Eris—the Goddess of Discord and Chaos. No doubt you've seen my likeness on the temple walls."

Sinbad regarded her. "You know, they don't do you justice, " he said. If you're going to die, die with some style, he figured.

"Mm-hmm," she agreed. "Now, about my sea monster . . ."

"Right. Right! Listen, I'm really, really sorry about that," said Sinbad, thinking on his feet, trying to charm her. "It's tough to lose a pet. I don't suppose a heartfelt apology would do?"

Amused to be sparring with Sinbad, Eris vanished into the shadowy recesses of the bubble. She reappeared moments later, human-sized, making their game more personal.

"'Heartfelt'? From you! Sinbad, you don't have a heart. And," she added, emerging from the shadows, "that's what I like about you. So I'm going to let you live. There's just one thing you have to do. Get the Book of Peace and bring it to me." She drew closer to Sinbad, her billowing hair almost enveloping him. Plucking the dagger from his belt, she traced it dangerously over his cheek.

"Right," he said, still thinking fast. "Now see, that's a problem, because I had my own plans for it. Ransom, get rich. . . you know, *me* stuff."

"You're not thinking big enough, Sinbad. Steal the Book for ransom and you'll be rich enough to lounge on an island beach. Steal the Book for me and you can buy the beach, and the island, and the world."

"You let me live," he said. "You make me rich. I retire to paradise. So far I don't see a downside. If you keep your word."

"Sinbad," she replied, "when a goddess gives her word, she's bound for all eternity." She casually crossed her heart, and a small glow appeared where she had touched her chest. It quickly disappeared.

"All right," he said. "You're on."

"I thought you'd see it my way," Eris murmured. Then she moved to the wall of the bubble, which she abruptly slashed with the dagger. A vision appeared, of a starry sky over the nighttime ocean. "When you've stolen the Book," she said, "follow that star beyond the horizon. You'll find yourself in Tartarus, my realm of Chaos."

Sinbad was still backing away. "Tartarus. See you there."

"It's a date, then. So, where were we?" she said. "Oh, yes. You were holding your breath."

Suddenly the air bubble burst, letting tons of seawater implode in on Sinbad, buffeting and tumbling him. In the swirling aftermath, he kicked desperately upward. At last he burst to the surface, gasping for air.

"He's so cute." Eris chuckled to herself as she swam away, well out of Sinbad's earshot. "And so gullible." She rejoined the sea monster. "Cetus, well done," she told him.

In moments, the *Chimera* came sailing up beside Sinbad. A massive hand reached down and seized him, lifting him bodily out of the water.

Kale dropped Sinbad unceremoniously onto the deck to the cheers of the crew.

Bets were settled all over the deck as Kale hauled Sinbad to his feet.

"Glad you made it," said Jin. He turned to Li. "Pay up," he snickered, "he lived."

"What happened down there?" Kale asked Sinbad.

"You wouldn't believe me if I told you," was the reply.

"Try me."

"All right. Here goes: I met Eris, the Goddess of Chaos. She's got a major crush on me and she invited me back to her place."

Kale gave him a deadpan look, and then burst into laughter. He reached out his gigantic arm and swatted Sinbad in approval of the joke. Sinbad reeled from the impact, hiding a grimace. "That's a good one," Kale roared. "Goddess of Chaos. I'm writing that down."

As Kale walked off, muttering to himself about Sinbad's joke, Rat dropped down from the rigging and landed next to Sinbad. "So, that's it, then," he said. "No Book. Now what do we do?"

"A little patience, Rat," said Sinbad. "It's not like we don't know where it's going."

Sinbad looked out at the royal flagship. The mainsail had just been replaced. It unfurled, and the flagship caught the wind and began to move away toward the horizon.

Up ahead, on the deck of the flagship, Proteus stood at the bow. "Men, all sails to Syracuse!" he commanded. Then he took one last backward glance toward Sinbad and the *Chimera*.

CHAPTER FOUR

he huge, majestic gates of Syracuse stood await-
ing the triumphal approach of the royal flagship. On deck, Proteus proudly strode toward
the forward bridge as the boat passed through the great
lock. Waterfalls gracefully descended on all sides as the
lock filled with water, carrying the ship upward with it.
A welcoming flock of white doves accompanied the
ship on its approach.

As Proteus reached the foredeck, the flagship com-
pleted its triumphant ascent. The gates opened, and
the breathtaking city of Syracuse was revealed. Before
the flagship lay the broad grand canal of Syracuse. It led
to the city's gleaming palace, its turrets and spires
reaching toward the heavens. The canal was lined with
what seemed to Proteus like the entire population of
the kingdom, cheering his arrival.

Aboard the flagship, the Book of Peace was brought
forth on an ornate litter. As the light from the Book

became visible, a joyous roar arose from the crowd.

Nearby, high above the grand canal, an elegant spire presided over the view. It was capped by an open rotunda flooded with light. This was the Book Tower, the specially built repository of the treasure that had been brought home by Proteus. It was there that the Book was now lovingly transported, past the cheering throng.

The royal citizens of Syracuse, accompanied by an honor guard, were present as the Book was placed atop a pedestal in the center of the solemn chamber. This would be home to the Book for the next one hundred years.

And then, later, it was time to celebrate. King Dymas, Proteus's father, was hosting a huge party for the city. The palace was a swirl of pageantry and costume as all the wellborn citizens of Syracuse gathered to share their joy at the return of the Book of Peace. They were joined by delegates from the other eleven cities, who treasured the Book's protection. The grand ballroom was crowded with excited revelers. Outside, on the large, romantic balcony that overlooked the city's glittering network of canals and architecture, a crowd of nobles and exotic dignitaries was cheering, laughing, and applauding at the sight of the illuminated tower. Above it all, the Book Tower glowed like the famed lighthouse at Alexandria.

Gray-bearded King Dymas, monarch of Syracuse, stood proudly among the nobility, a smile on his face. At his side was his son Proteus, and Proteus's betrothed, the beautiful Lady Marina. She wore a stunning sea-blue gown and a golden tiara.

The king was a formidable and distinguished man, yet he was still able to project a disarming and informal manner. It was obvious that his people loved him. "For as long as I can remember," he told the assembled group, "I've dreamed of this moment. The sacred treasure that's protected us for a thousand years is now in Syracuse."

As he spoke, Dymas gave special deference to the Delegation of the Twelve Cities. The lead delegate, wise and weary, stood beside Dymas.

They raised their glasses for a toast. "To the Book of Peace!" Dymas said.

"And to you, King Dymas!" added the lead delegate. The crowd cheered as the delegates of the Twelve Cities eagerly raised their glasses higher and offered congratulations to the king.

"Well spoken, King Dymas!" they cried. "Thank you, Your Majesty!"

Public duties done, Dymas gathered his beloved Proteus under an arm and walked with him and Lady Marina through the parting crowd to the ballroom inside.

"Congratulations, Father," said Proteus.

At the center of the ballroom, a spectacular flame was ignited, sending an elegant balloon floating upward. The orchestra struck up a tune, and a large reception greeted the king and prince.

Suddenly, a guard brushed past Dymas, rushing for the door. Dymas and Proteus looked after him, and saw that a commotion was beginning to stir at the ballroom entrance.

At the door, two guards in ceremonial uniform, who had been greeting guests as they filed into the ballroom, suddenly drew their swords and whirled to block the entrance.

The commotion at the door had now gathered the attention of the party crowd in the ballroom. The elite of Syracuse reacted with curiosity and then alarm. Whoever had arrived at the front entrance had stopped the party cold. Even the orchestra faltered into silence.

There stood Sinbad, in a standoff with the belligerent guards. With him were Kale, Rat, and Jed.

"See, this is what happens when you use the front entrance," Sinbad said to Kale.

Dymas and Proteus moved forward and saw Sinbad beyond the guards. Proteus smiled.

"What is he doing here?" Dymas asked his son with concern.

"At least he's not out robbing someone," Proteus replied.

"That's because everyone worth robbing is here," said Dymas.

Proteus stepped toward the commotion. He gestured at the orchestra leader, and the music started again.

Sinbad smiled as he saw Proteus approaching from behind the guards. "I'll bet you guys ten crowns you're about to put those swords down," he said to the guards.

"I'll take that bet," one of them said confidently.

Proteus walked up behind them. "Guards, put away your swords," he ordered.

They grimaced and reluctantly obeyed.

"You can pay me later," Sinbad told the guards as he pushed their swords out of the way. He made his way toward Proteus, and the two shared a hearty handshake, grinning widely.

"I don't see you for ten years," Proteus said, "and now twice in one day. You're smothering me!" He laughed.

"I knew you'd want to thank me for saving your life. . . Again."

"You probably just heard we had free food and wine," said Proteus.

"You hear that, guys?" Sinbad said to his crew. "Dinner and drinks are on the prince!" Quietly, so nobody else could hear, he added, "Get to work."

Proteus pulled Sinbad into the ballroom. "C'mon, there's someone I want you to meet."

Kale, Rat, and Jed, following Sinbad, moved to pass the guards, who once again blocked their entrance.

"Weapons?" inquired a guard.

Kale removed two knives from the back of his sash, and placed them on a table to the side of the door. Rat removed his machete. Then they strode into the party, though they had to leave Jed, who was pulling a seemingly endless stream of knives, bolos, garrotes, and boomerangs out of various pockets.

Like herring scattering before prowling sharks, the partygoers avoided Sinbad and Proteus as they strolled through the ballroom. Proteus led Sinbad toward Marina, who was facing away from them.

"Here she is," Proteus told his guest. "I've told her all about you. Sinbad, I would like to introduce you to my fiancée, the Lady Marina, Ambassador from Thrace."

As Proteus was in mid-introduction, she turned toward them, and all at once Sinbad looked as if his world had just flipped upside down. He knew her. He had seen her once, a long, long time ago. Marina smiled, obviously never having met Sinbad before.

"Oh, so this is the infamous Sinbad," Marina said. "I heard all about you this morning. First you try to rob Proteus, then you save his life. So which are you, a thief or a hero?"

There was an awkward pause, and finally Proteus spoke up to break the difficult moment. "Sinbad came to give me an opportunity to thank . . . him—" he said, stopping in midsentence as he turned toward Sinbad and realized that he was gone. Marina and Proteus just looked at each other in puzzlement.

Nearby, Rat was monopolizing a servant who was bearing trays of food, stuffing canapés into all his pockets. "Eight months on the sea with nothing but eggs and pickles—you don't know what that can do to a man," he said feverishly. Then he looked up to see Sinbad stalking past him toward the door. He scurried after his leader, cramming the last handfuls of food into his clothes. Near the door, he darted eagerly between Kale and Sinbad. "It's almost too easy," he said through a mouthful of sausage. "There's only a handful of guards."

"Forget it," said Sinbad. "Let's get back to the ship."

"Just like that?" said Kale. "But the Book is almost ours."

Kale looked past Sinbad and spotted Marina through the crowd. As soon as he saw her, he alone understood Sinbad's strange behavior. "Oh," he said quickly.

"What?" said Rat. "Old girlfriend or something?"

"Afraid it's not as simple as that," Kale replied. "Let's go."

Kale followed after Sinbad as Rat looked back into the crowd, trying to figure out what had just happened. Finally he gave up and followed behind them, muttering.

At the ballroom entrance, Jed had just finished

adding the last of his weapons to the tower of deadly toys on the table when Sinbad strode past the guards with Rat and Kale in tow. "Pack it up," Kale said to Jed.

"What? But—I just— Argh," Jed sputtered. He scooped up the blades and throwing stars into his arms and hustled to catch up.

The shadows of Sinbad's group flickered on the walls as they passed the fiery lanterns at the ballroom entrance. As the crew departed, the shadows remained, forming into the looming face of Eris. She smiled and clapped her hands. "This is just too easy," she said.

She vanished like a gust, leaving the guards at the entrance to wonder at the sudden breeze.

A little later, Marina and Proteus walked out into the palace gardens, laughing together. "Look at it this way," Marina said. "Now that Sinbad's gone, your father can finally relax and enjoy the evening."

"Well, you're right about that," he agreed. "He's trying not to show it, but he's so proud to have the Book in Syracuse. He's been planning this day his whole life."

They stopped at a beautiful cliff overlooking the ocean. In the distance they could see the tower, gloriously illuminated by the light from the Book of Peace.

"Soon it'll be your responsibility," said Marina.

"*Our* responsibility," Proteus reminded her.

She smiled, gazing out over the ocean. "It's beautiful," she said wistfully.

Proteus was looking at the tower. "It is," he agreed. "My father spent years preparing it for the Book. There are guards on every level, and if you look up to—" He stopped, realizing that Marina was smiling at him. "You were talking about the ocean, weren't you?"

She looked over the waves, longing in her eyes. "I only wish I'd seen more of it. I used to imagine sailing far beyond the Twelve Cities, discovering the world. Ah, look at it, Proteus. So much wonder."

Proteus only looked at Marina, hearing the longing in her voice. "Marina. . . our marriage was arranged many years ago. It's always been expected of us." They sat down on a large rock. "But politics is not a reason to get married," he continued, "and I don't want you to do this just because it's your duty."

Marina looked concerned. She could feel the honesty behind Proteus's words.

"I'm asking you for myself now," he said. "Marina, will you marry me?"

"Proteus, I . . ."

Before she could answer, a shadow fell over them. They turned to see Dymas approaching. "There you are!" he said to Marina. "I think the Manolians want to give a toast—although I'm not sure—" He grew a bit flustered. "They're doing something with their knees."

Dymas reached for Marina's hand. "I need an ambassador," he concluded.

Marina looked at Proteus. He smiled.

"Of course, Sire," she said, smiling at Dymas. She took the king's arm, and Proteus's, and walked with them into the palace.

CHAPTER FIVE

*M*eanwhile, in the high tower overlooking the city, a lone guard patrolled the sacred chamber. The music from the celebration could be heard faintly.

There was a tiny sound, and a shadow crossed the room. A gust of wind blew out a nearby lamp. Suspicious, the guard approached. It was quiet again. He sheathed his sword and looked down at the Book.

He smiled, his face lit by the magical, golden light that shone from the Book. He could not see that behind him, on the floor, his own shadow was growing, changing shape, becoming . . . Eris.

Her shadowy hands covered the chamber's other two lamps, extinguishing them. Spooked, the guard spun around, drawing his sword. "Who's there?" he cried.

Eris slithered to the far side of a marble column. She blew on her hands, and before her, a smoky mask of a face appeared. It was Sinbad. She pulled the mask over her own face—and became Sinbad. Her plan was set in motion.

The shadowy figure of Sinbad stepped out from behind the pillar as the guard turned and saw him. "You!" he shouted.

The shadow Sinbad drew a dagger and stepped forward menacingly, eyes glowing.

"Sinbad!" said the guard. He lunged forward, putting all his force behind the swing of his sword and—*clang!* The shadow Sinbad stopped it cold, and then struck the stunned guard full in the face with a mighty blow. He was out before he hit the floor.

With supreme confidence, the shadow Sinbad swaggered past the fallen guard, and the veil-like Sinbad disguise melted away like a lifting fog to reveal Eris. She looked quite satisfied with her work. "I love playing pretend," she said aloud as she dropped the dagger—*Sinbad*'s dagger—onto the floor in front of the guard. It was the very dagger that Eris had taken from Sinbad after Cetus had dragged him down under the sea. Eris laughed with satisfaction at her own cleverness as she swirled toward the Book.

When she reached the Book pedestal, Eris paused to savor the moment. The light from the Book itself had intensified and taken on a shimmering, energized quality.

Eris gathered it up. Victoriously, she held the Book

above her head. Then, with a vicious grin, she slammed it closed.

"All the pieces are coming together," she gloated.

With one great flash, the light went out. The pedestal disintegrated, smashed to smithereens, as Eris disappeared.

Moments later, in the great ballroom, the huge chandelier shook as the domed ceiling above it cracked and shuddered. Debris fell among the guests, who ran for cover. As Dymas was pulled out of danger by his guards, Marina and Proteus ran together out to the balcony.

Horrified, they looked up to see a huge, dark cloud issuing from the Book Tower, blanketing the city. "Proteus—the Book," gasped Marina.

The buildings of Syracuse continued to shake and crack as the cloud covered the night sky.

A short while later, a jail-cell door burst open, and a struggling Sinbad was thrown inside by the palace guards. He rolled onto his feet as the guards departed.

"Sinbad," said a tense voice from the darkness in the cell.

"Proteus!" cried Sinbad in relief. "It's about time—"

Proteus did not let him finish. "Do you realize how serious this is?" he yelled.

"Do you realize how many times I've heard that

today?" Sinbad shot back at him, frustrated.

"You betrayed Syracuse!"

"Ah, not you, too," said Sinbad.

Proteus loomed over him. "Stealing the Book of Peace when you knew how much it'meant to us," he said.

"Proteus, here's the way this works: first I actually commit the crime and then you get to blame me for it." Now he was really getting irritated.

"How do you explain this?" Proteus demanded. He held up Sinbad's dagger.

Sinbad took a moment as he realized the gravity of his situation. "Eris," he whispered to himself. How was he going to get out of this?

"What?" Proteus said.

"She framed me for this!"

Proteus walked away from him. "Sinbad—listen to yourself!" he said in disgust. He couldn't believe Sinbad would lie about something so important.

"Trust me, Proteus," said Sinbad, "that Book is in Tartarus. Get some noble sap to go there and get it back. Simple as that. Talk to your father, tell him—"

Turning, Proteus cut him off. "This is beyond my father. The ambassadors are convening now for your trial."

"Whoa, whoa, whoa—*trial*? I didn't do it! I left the Book on your ship and that's the last I saw of it! You were there! You know the truth! You know me!"

"Do I?" asked Proteus. "I knew a kid. Who are you now, Sinbad? Look me in the eye and tell me: Did you steal the Book?"

"No."

Proteus stared at him for a moment, and then walked out of the cell.

In the palace throne room, King Dymas stood before a long podium, behind which delegates from the Twelve Cities were arrayed to sit in judgement. Sinbad stood in chains before them.

"We've heard enough of your lies," Dymas exclaimed. "Sinbad, for the last time, give us the Book!"

"How many times do I have to tell you? I don't have it!" Sinbad retorted.

"Very well, then," said one of the ambassadors. "The Delegation of the Twelve Cities finds you guilty of treason and we sentence you to die. Take him away."

Sinbad struggled with the guards as they tried to lead him away, still pleading his innocence. "C'mon—this is a joke, right? You're making a mistake. Are you people blind? I didn't do it!"

"*Stop!*" shouted a voice from the back of the room.

Everyone turned to look. It was Proteus, making his way forward through the crowd! Shocked, Marina stood up. She couldn't believe what he was doing. The crowd murmured as Proteus moved to stand near Sinbad.

King Dymas stepped forward.

"I demand the right of substitution," Proteus said loudly. The crowd gasped in horror and confusion. "Take me in his place," Proteus continued.

"No!" cried Dymas. What was his son thinking?

"Sinbad says that Eris took the Book, and I believe him," Proteus said, looking at Sinbad. "Let him go to Tartarus and recover it."

"*What?*" said Sinbad, as surprised as the stunned crowd of onlookers.

The delegates began to whisper intensely to one another.

"What are you doing?" Sinbad said to Proteus.

"You claim that Eris stole the Book," said Proteus, grabbing hold of Sinbad's shirt. "Steal it back!"

As the crowd watched, he pushed Sinbad away. "You're good at that," he finished. He stalked away from Sinbad.

Sinbad grabbed onto Proteus to stop him. "Hey, look—I will not be responsible for your life!" he said.

"You would do the same for me," Proteus replied.

"No. I wouldn't," Sinbad stated flatly.

King Dymas turned from the delegates and approached his son, pleading. "If Sinbad is allowed to leave the city, he'll never come back! Son, listen to reason."

"No, Father, you listen. Sinbad either stole the Book, or he's telling the truth and it's in Tartarus. Either way, he's our only hope."

Now the ambassador who was leader of the delegation held up his hand to stop the debate. "Proteus," he said, "you realize that if Sinbad does not return, you will be put to death in his place."

"I understand."

"So be it. Sinbad has ten days to return the Book." The delegates had spoken.

Dymas could barely control his frustration and shock. But he collected himself as he remembered his duties as leader of Syracuse. He turned to the guards holding Sinbad. "Release him," he ordered sadly.

Sinbad's chains were removed, and the guards put handcuffs on Proteus.

As they led him out of the chamber, Proteus looked over his shoulder at Sinbad. "Oh, and Sinbad," he said. "Don't be late."

Marina glared at Sinbad in disgust, and then followed Proteus out.

CHAPTER SIX

The next morning before dawn, the outer gates of Syracuse opened and the *Chimera* was carried on a gentle wave out into the ocean. High above the deck, Rat swung across from the yardarm, a lit torch between his teeth, lighting lamps around the ship. Rat reached Kale, and a lantern beside the first mate flared to life.

Kale closely studied a chart in front of him. Sinbad stood nearby at the stern, studying Eris's star as it flickered in the distance.

"So," said Kale, "any idea how we actually get to Tartarus?"

Sinbad turned to look at Kale. "Tartarus? People get killed in Tartarus," he said.

"So where are we going?" Kale asked him.

Sinbad slammed a chart down in front of Kale. "Fiji!"

Kale was surprised. "Fiji? This time of year?"

"Think of the beaches."

"Beautiful," said Kale. "If you like mosquitoes."

"Think of the sun."

"It's monsoon season," Kale countered. He hadn't forgotten Sinbad's obligation to Proteus.

"Well, then, the women."

"They're cannibals, Sinbad."

"Exactly!" said Sinbad. He let that one hang for a second, expecting Kale to come around. But his first mate wasn't in the mood for a joke. There was no response.

Sinbad followed him. "C'mon, Kale—"

"He's your friend," Kale said, really mad now.

"Listen to you! You sound like my mother! Proteus will be fine."

"You're sure of that?"

"You and I both know Dymas isn't going to let them execute his only son," said Sinbad.

Kale stared defiantly at Sinbad. "So, we're running away?" he challenged.

"We're retiring. We don't need another score. We've got enough. Now, set a course for Fiji!" Sinbad commanded.

Kale was unconvinced. He spun the wheel angrily, still drilling Sinbad with his glare.

Sinbad ignored him. He headed for his cabin, shouting to his men: "Gentlemen, we're heading to Fiji!" The crew cheered.

Sinbad stomped down the stairs to his cabin, the

cheers of his men echoing behind him. "Darn Kale," he muttered to himself. "Darn Book. Darn Proteus."

When he got inside his cabin, there was a figure standing over his map table, sorting through his belongings.

It was Marina. She looked much more comfortable now, not wearing an evening gown but instead a rough seafarer's outfit. Nevertheless, despite the common clothing, she still looked very good.

"Look at all this," she was muttering to herself.

Sinbad ducked quickly out of the cabin, shocked. He took a second to compose himself, watching Marina as she inspected one of his trophies. It was the fragile skull of a gorgon.

"Oh, but this can't be real," she said softly. "It would be too deli—" A piece snapped off in her hand. "—cate," she finished. She hastily replaced the broken piece and continued looking around, not hearing Sinbad as he came into the cabin.

"This is more like it," she said, holding up an ornate dagger as he walked up quietly behind her. "Stolen from Venezia," she mused. Next she regarded a metal amulet. "From Pompeii," she said to herself. "And," she said, holding up a bejeweled bra, "from a brothel in Syracuse."

"Good guess," said Sinbad behind her.

She dropped it, startled, and turned to face him.

"What do you think you're doing here?" he asked her.

"I'm here to make sure you get the Book of Peace—or bring back your dead body if you fail," she told him fiercely.

"And how are you gonna pull that off?" he asked, a wicked gleam in his eye.

"By whatever means necessary."

"Really," he said. "Did you bring a crew?"

"No," she admitted.

"You know how to get to Tartarus?" he asked.

"No."

"Can you navigate on your own?" He smiled at her now.

"Yes!" she said, happy to have something she could answer positively to.

He pounced. "Well, good. Then I'll dump your butt in a rowboat and you can paddle all the way back to Syracuse, 'cause we're going to Fiji."

He jumped onto his bed, leaned back, and pulled his turban down over his eyes. As far as he was concerned, the conversation was over and he had won.

"Fiji," said Marina.

"Yep."

"Just as I thought."

"What?" said Sinbad.

"Sinbad, you're not a very complicated guy—all someone has to do is imagine the most gutless course of action and you're bound to take it."

"Hey, this is not my problem," he said defensively. "I didn't steal the Book."

"You're really not going to lose any sleep over this, are you?" said Marina.

"Not a wink."

"Because, me," she said, "I'd be tossing and turning, knowing I'm alive because I let my friend die."

That one hit Sinbad. He sat up in his bunk, irritated and cornered. Marina walked away, with Sinbad quick on her heels. "I'm not responsible for this mess, and I didn't ask Proteus to put his neck on the line for me," he argued.

"Clearly I can't appeal to your 'honor,'" she said, making little quotes with her fingers. "But I have other ways of convincing you."

"Oh, really. Just how do you expect to do that?"

"By speaking your language," said Marina, abruptly producing a fantastic jewel. Sinbad couldn't help but be impressed. But, flustered and defensive, he adopted a skeptical demeanor.

"Keep talking," he told her.

Marina brought out a velvet bag and emptied it without a word into Sinbad's open palm. Two more glittering gems fell out.

Sinbad studied the precious stones. "Hmm. This'll do," he said at last, being sure not to look impressed.

"But not for first class," he added.

Marina's smile vanished. She knew what was coming.

Moments later, Sinbad's door burst open. Yelling and struggling, Marina fought angrily as Sinbad carried her like a sack of potatoes across the deck. The *Chimera* crew looked up at them but kept working, pretending to ignore the commotion.

"As you can see," said Sinbad, laughing wickedly, "we're well equipped to accommodate the most discerning of royal tastes. We have excellent ocean views—"

His guided tour was cut off as Marina grabbed his turban and yanked his head back. Unfazed, he headed toward a storage room. "Luxurious living quarters," he announced. He flipped the still-fighting Marina around into his arms, kicked open the storage-room door, and dropped her onto a stack of supplies. "With three gourmet meals a day: pickles, eggs, and . . . pickles!"

As Sinbad laughed, Spike the dog pushed past them into the storage area. He was mangy and escorted by flies. And, as always, he was slobbering enthusiastically.

"Oh, hey, Spike. There you are," said Sinbad cheerfully. He turned to Marina. "I'd like to introduce you to your new bunkmate," he said to her. "Well, actually, you're his new bunkmate, as it's actually his bunk."

Spike happily climbed into Marina's lap and licked her face. She groaned.

"We hope you have a pleasant stay aboard the

Chimera," said Sinbad, starting to leave. Then he popped his head back in again. "Oh," he added, "if he starts hugging your leg, it means he likes you."

"If you think you—" Marina yelled at his back as he left, but he slammed the door, cutting her off.

When Sinbad emerged from belowdecks, he was studying the gem in his hand, scowling. "How did she even get on the ship?" he muttered to himself.

He looked up and immediately got his answer, as the rest of his crew were regarding gems of their own. The men, seeing him, tucked their jewels away and got busy fast. So that was it.

He stalked past Jin, Li, and Jed. "Gentlemen," he told the crew, "we have a new course. We're going to Tartarus."

"What happened to Fiji?" Jin wanted to know.

"No fun? No beaches?" Li moaned.

A coil of rope fell on Sinbad from above. "Rat!" yelped Sinbad.

"Sorry, Captain!" Rat shouted down from the crow's nest. Then he dropped down beside Sinbad. "But did you say Tartarus?"

"That's right," said Sinbad crabbily over his shoulder as he walked away. He hated it that Marina had gotten to him. But she had definitely won.

Sinbad continued his march, but Rat again dropped down right in front of him. "Would that be the same

Sinbad and the crew of the *Chimera*.

Under attack!

Sinbad's old friend Proteus guards the
Book of Peace.

Marina stows away on Sinbad's ship.

SINBAD
LEGEND OF THE SEVEN SEAS

Sinbad and his faithful sidekick, Spike.

The Sirens hypnotize the crew of the *Chimera*.

Marina tries to coax Sinbad out from under the Sirens' spell.

Spike helps save the ship from the danger
of the Dragon's Teeth.

The crew backs away as
Fish Island comes to life!

The *Chimera* crew prepares for
the ride of their lives.

MARINA
AMBASSADOR FROM THRACE

The terrifying Roc, sent by Eris,
chases Sinbad and Marina.

A slippery escape from the
Roc's clutches.

Sinbad and Marina are cofronted by Eris's monsters.

Proteus braves the fate meant for Sinbad.

ERIS
EVIL GODDESS OF CHAOS

Eris must concede defeat.

With the Book of Peace returned to Syracuse, Marina rejoins Sinbad aboard the *Chimera*.

SPIKE

OFFICIAL MASCOT OF THE *CHIMERA*

Tartarus from which no sailor ever returns?" Rat asked. "The Tartarus of lost souls, where they grind your bones and pickle your spleen?"

Sinbad smiled at Rat, who was now hanging upside down in front of his face. "No, Rat, this is the nice Tartarus with gobs of beaches and drinks—you know, with the little umbrellas?"

Sinbad kept walking, while behind him, Rat scowled. "*Non ci posso credere, non ci posso credere, mi hanno fregato ancora,*" he muttered in frustration. "I cannot believe, I cannot believe, they tricked me again."

Sinbad continued up to the top deck, where Kale was still at the wheel. The first mate stared straight ahead, his face expressionless. Sinbad glared at him for a second, then turned to stare in the same direction.

"Mm-hmm," said Kale smugly.

"I'm only doing this for the money," said Sinbad, fooling no one.

A hint of a smile crossed Kale's face. "Right," he said. "So, how do we get there?"

Sinbad pointed to Eris's star on the horizon. "That star's our point."

Kale gave the wheel a hearty push and the *Chimera* bit into the waves and swung around for the star. A gust of wind snapped the sails full, and the ship surged across the smooth blue ocean toward the horizon.

Far, far, above, Eris was watching with interest. She wore a glittering sequined evening gown that flowed into starry spiral arms, and stood in the center of a glorious sweep of the celestial cosmos. In her hands she held a champagne glass, and in the glass was the blue ocean itself, the *Chimera* a tiny dot upon it. She blew gently on the surface of the champagne sea, and the little ship's sails filled, making the craft move faster. Her menagerie of constellation monsters gathered around her to watch.

"So," she said, "our little thief isn't going to run away. He thinks he's going to pay us a visit. Let's provide some mood music."

With her finger, Eris gently swirled the rim of her cocktail glass, creating a whining sound. Swimming female forms began taking shape in the spinning liquid.

As a distant voice was heard singing, Eris smiled in satisfaction.

CHAPTER SEVEN

Outside Spike's "cabin," a dagger slid through a crack in the door, prying the pin from one of the hinges. It clattered to the floor beside several others. Then Marina kicked the door down. She was free.

Spike slunk out next, looking humiliated. Marina had tied big ribbon bows onto his ears

"Oh, come on. You look great," she chided him.

When Marina emerged from belowdecks, she could see the crew dashing about, preparing for something.

Kale was shouting orders: "Look lively! Jed! Get the longpoles!"

Marina ducked and turned to avoid a swinging line, and turned again to dodge Jed, who was rushing by. "Pardon me, m'lady," he said.

Then Marina looked up. A shadow of worry crossed her face. They were sailing into a narrow channel that was wedged between a set of huge, threatening rock pinnacles. The ship was dwarfed beneath them.

"The Dragon's Teeth," Marina said under her breath, looking both awed and terrified.

Above her, Rat cleared his throat. Marina looked up at the sound, and then shrank back as Rat dove downward and hung upside down in front of her.

"Indeed, *signorina*," said Rat, "only the most foolish of captains would dare to sail a ship through—"

"Rat!" Sinbad called from the wheel, interrupting him. "Reef the foresail!"

"Oh—excuse me, *signorina*," said Rat. With a wink, he disappeared again.

Marina turned and hurried to Sinbad. "Are you sure you—" she began.

Sinbad cut her off. "Yes, we've done this kind of thing before," he said curtly.

"Look—" she tried again.

"No, there is no other way."

"But—"

"And yes," said Sinbad, "you have my permission to stand there quietly and get a free lesson in sailing." Marina, doing a slow burn, was about to tell Sinbad where he could stick his sailing lesson, when Sinbad continued. "Besides—a ship is no place for a woman."

Marina groaned in disbelief. Where could she even *start* with a man like him?

Sinbad shouted to the main deck. "Jin! Easy on the main!"

"Aye!" Jin answered from below.

The *Chimera* continued moving into the huge jagged rocks. Marina's face darkened in shadow as the ship continued its careful progress through the channel of the towering Dragon's Teeth.

"Steady as she goes," Sinbad called to his crew.

It was eerily quiet.

Then, from up in the crow's nest, Rat shouted down a warning: "Rocks—off the starboard bow!"

Standing tensely, Sinbad corrected their course. At the bow, Luca, one of the crewmen, peered into the fog, and pointed at something ahead of them.

Now Sinbad and Marina could see the wreckage of a ship, partially submerged in the water before them. Out of the fog, like ghosts, other strange, destroyed boats emerged to surround them. Sinbad and Marina looked around in stunned wonder at the wrecked and desolate hulls, some of them still impaled atop the sharp towers of stone. As they passed under the prow of one wreck, water dripped down the face of its figurehead. The wooden statue of a beautiful woman on the front of the boat that had, in better times, proudly led its ship over the swelling ocean now looked as if it were weeping.

Then Marina began to hear it: a strange noise, like a voice. Then there were other voices, faint but growing louder.

"Steady . . . " said Sinbad quietly.

"What is that sound?" asked Marina, chilled to the bone.

"Shhh," said Sinbad. He seemed to be in a bit of a daze.

Marina peered into the fog, and then she saw them: the Sirens.

From the shipwrecks in the *Chimera*'s wake, strange watery female shapes began slipping free from the wooden figureheads, sliding into the water to follow the *Chimera.*

Marina had a bad feeling. She turned to Sinbad. "Sinbad, I—"

The sound grew louder and more mesmerizing. Jumping up on the side rail, Spike began to bark, his hackles raised. Marina hurried to look over the side. The strange figures were now moving swiftly under the surface of the water, converging on the *Chimera.*

And then, they leaped from the water, singing their hypnotic song. They were beautiful and yet horrible. They laughed menacingly.

Spike growled, and Marina ran back to Sinbad and put her hand on his shoulder. "Sinbad?" she said, trying to shake him from the daze he had fallen into.

She was nearly knocked off her feet as the boat's hull smacked against a rock in the channel. The *Chimera* was now moving down the rapids.

"*Sinbad?*" Marina said again, more urgently. But Sinbad was transfixed by the Sirens.

Marina looked around her and saw that the crew had abandoned their posts. She ran up to the them, one by one, and tried to rouse them: "Jin? Li?"

It was no use. They were all wandering the deck in a stupor. They were intoxicated, entranced, spellbound—seduced by the strange, haunting Sirens' song. Only Marina, because she was a woman, was immune, along with Spike.

"Come and get it, ladies," said Luca.

"Kale?" Marina begged the first mate, hoping that he, of all of them, would be able to keep his head.

"Come with me, we'll speak of love," said Kale, looking at her but not seeing her. He, too, had been hypnotized by the treacherous beings.

Marina looked up to see the *Chimera* rushing toward a huge outcropping of rocks. In desperation, she turned to Sinbad, who was still in a fog, hearing only the Sirens' call. A silly grin was on his face. She grabbed him and shook him. He was useless—and difficult to budge. Struggling, Marina pulled Sinbad's legs out from under him and pushed him aside as best she could, as the *Chimera* careened off another rock with a tremendous crunch. She grabbed the wheel, barely managing to steer the ship away from the edge of a waterfall that lay ahead.

Spike whimpered in concern as he looked into Sinbad's unseeing eyes.

The Sirens rose up before the prow of the boat like a tidal wave, beautiful and seductive and totally malicious. They were in high spirits, laughing, singing, and calling to the men to join them.

The enchanted crewmen staggered toward the Sirens, who reached out their watery arms and beckoned the men to the frigid depths of the ocean. As they reached for the temptresses, a wave crashed over them, knocking them to the deck.

"Who's bad? Sin-bad!" said Sinbad, still lying on the deck in his stupor and dreaming of love.

The men scrambled to their feet, even more intent on the Sirens. Jin rudely pushed his brother aside to get to one of them.

"Ugh—men," muttered Marina, looking at them in pity.

She had to do something. If she didn't, no one would. Marina looked around wildly and spotted a rope coiled on the deck. Breathless, she grabbed its end and put it between Spike's teeth. "Round the deck!" she ordered the dog. "Now!"

Spike, pulling the rope after him, raced around the crewmen, tying them up in a bunch and yanking them back from the clutches of the Sirens.

Wailing angrily, the Sirens dove back into the waves.

"*Mi amore!*" called a voice from above. Marina looked up just in time to see an entranced Rat leaping from the crow's nest. "My darling!" he cried. He landed near the prow and, rope in one hand, leaned dangerously out over the water, reaching out to his beloved.

"Rat!" yelled Marina.

"I love you!" Rat called, unable to hear Marina. The Siren loomed up out of the waves to kiss him. "*Amore, amore, amore*, my love, my love, my darling, I love you. *Si, tra il mare a le onde andiamo via.* Yes, between the sea and the waves we go away." As Rat kissed the watery Siren, the rope slipped through his hand and he fell overboard.

Desperate, Marina hauled Sinbad up off the deck and used his deadweight to steady the wheel. She grabbed a hook with a rope tied to it, threw it over the yardarm, and swung it out over the water. Hooking the drowning Rat by his trousers, she landed back on the deck and hauled mightily on the rope to fish Rat out of the ocean.

Rat's Siren now flew by Sinbad, who was instantly hypnotized by her and stumbled off in pursuit. Marina looked up from rescuing Rat just in time to see Sinbad, dangerously close to going overboard after his lovely Siren.

"*Spike! Get Sinbad!*" she yelled urgently.

Spike charged Sinbad, who yelped as the huge dog bit down on the seat of his pants and pulled, tearing a big hole. That didn't stop Sinbad, though. He staggered away again, right into the arms of another Siren, who started to kiss him.

As the ship plunged over a waterfall, Marina slid and rolled down the deck. With a yell, she crashed right through the Siren, who disappeared with a splash. Now it was Marina in Sinbad's arms.

Still thinking she was the Siren, he lay a big kiss on her. Disgusted, Marina hit him with a right hook that sent him sprawling across the deck.

Marina had no time to waste. She looked ahead to see that the *Chimera* was sailing straight into another mountain of jagged rocks, surrounded by the wrecks of other ships. She raced back to the wheel.

Sinbad got up slowly from the deck, still dazed. Marina took hold of the wheel. The Sirens, laughing evilly, beckoned her toward the jagged pinnacles of rock, where they cavorted and leaped onto the wreckage, hoping to seal the fate of the *Chimera* and all aboard.

Marina took this all in, and then, with a determined look, turned the wheel hard. She was heading directly toward the wreck of another ship.

"Spike!" Marina yelled. "The blades!"

Spike ran right over Sinbad on his way to do Marina's bidding. He kicked the lever, and the blades shot out from the sides of the *Chimera*. With the sharp metal slicing through the wood, the *Chimera* skidded across the wreckage and was thrust up into the air.

The Sirens cried out in anger and frustration as the *Chimera* ran straight at them, blades extended—reducing them to water again. Flying over the rocks, the *Chimera* landed with a thunderous splash in the calm, open water on the other side. And then, hundreds of flying fish burst up through the water around the ship. The *Chimera* was free.

Marina got up slowly, watching the flying fish move off. Smiling, she took the helm. On the deck below her, Sinbad got to his feet as well, still a bit dazed. Behind him, his crew was regaining its senses. He looked around, taking in the calm scene.

As his head cleared, he noticed Marina standing at the wheel. She was at ease, completely in control. She looked good. He stared at her. He rubbed his hand slowly across his face. Then he walked toward her, past his men.

"Ugh . . . wha happened?" said Jed, shaking his head.

Hasaan, not back to normal, was holding a fish and regarding it rapturously. "Oh, my precious . . ." he said to it.

"Wake up, you eedgit," said another sailor, Chum.

Rat swung through, hanging upside down, causing everyone to duck.

"Sinbad saved us," mumbled Jin groggily, trying to put the pieces together.

Rat swung past once more. "No," he said happily. "Marina!"

"Marina saved us!" . . . "Marina?" . . . "Marina!" mumbled the dazed members of the *Chimera* crew.

Hearing this, Sinbad grimaced and continued across the deck toward Marina. Wagging his tail, a very happy Spike led Sinbad up the stairs to Marina. The dog trotted up to her. "Hey, if it isn't my little hero!" she said, patting Spike's head and making a big fuss over him. "You were so brave! What a good dog!"

As Marina continued to shower attention on Spike, Sinbad scratched his head, trying to find a way to begin. To say thank you.

To Marina.

"Uh . . . " he said, clearing his throat.

Marina turned toward him, smiling. "Still think a ship's no place for a woman?" she said.

He looked at her. It was obvious what he was thinking: I can't thank *her*!

"Urrgh. . . Absolutely!" Sinbad stammered. He gestured in frustration. "I mean . . . Look at my ship!"

Marina stared at him in disbelief as he continued his rant, digging himself deeper. "This railing was hand-carved mahogany!" he said, making a big deal out of examining the damage. "And here—these moldings came all the way from Damascus—do you have any idea what I went through to steal these?" He turned back to her. "That's exactly why women shouldn't drive!" he finished up.

"Are you crazy?" said Marina, thoroughly exasperated. "I saved your life!"

Sinbad closed the distance between them quickly, pulled her hand from the wheel with a dismissive gesture, and took her place at the helm. "Oh, I would have been fine. I always am," he said airily.

Marina knew better. She had seen him hypnotized by the Sirens, a goofy grin plastered across his face. She turned on her heel and stomped away. "Right!" she yelled. Down the stairs she marched, across the deck past the watching crewmen, and headed for her "cabin."

Sinbad watched her for a moment. Then he noticed something on the side of the ship and did a fast double take. "And—you chipped the paint!" he shouted after her.

Marina stopped in her tracks. Then she opened her cabin door dramatically, just waiting for him to finish.

"Right here! Look at that! Look at that! That's more than a little scratch!" he ranted. When he was done, Marina made a disgusted sound and slammed the door behind her.

The men all turned and looked at Sinbad, who stood at the wheel with hunched shoulders and a sour look on his face. Even these rough seamen were shocked by his bad manners. Spike watched him, flattened his ears, and growled.

Sinbad heaved an exasperated sigh. He knew he was acting like an idiot. Finally, the tension got to be too much. He turned and stomped down to Marina's storage room, Spike at his heels.

"Darn dog," he grumbled. "Darn crew . . . Darn woman . . . " He pounded on the door and stood back, arms across his chest.

Nothing happened.

Scowling, Sinbad looked around. Everyone had stopped what they were doing to watch the rare sight of Sinbad apologizing.

He pounded harder on the door, until finally she flung it open. "*WHAT!*" Marina yelled.

"*Thank you!*" Sinbad yelled back.

"*You're welcome!*"

"*No problem!*"

"*Don't worry about it!*" Marina shouted.

"*I WON'T!*"

"*GOOD!*"

"*G'BYE!*"

"*BYE TO YOU!*" yelled Marina, and slammed the door shut again.

Sinbad turned and looked at his crew. They moved off quickly, feigning disinterest. Scowling, he looked back at the door. He smiled, just a little. When he glanced at Spike, he went back to the scowl. "Ya happy now?" he asked Spike. Spike wagged his tail.

Sinbad made a disgusted sound. As he walked back up to the top deck, the crew noticed the gaping hole in the seat of his pants. They enjoyed a silent chuckle behind Sinbad's back.

CHAPTER EIGHT

The *Chimera* sailed over the moonlit waves, steadily following Eris's star. The moon's reflection shone brightly on the water.

The same bright moon hung over Syracuse that night. Proteus stood at his cell window, gazing at its image shimmering over the ocean outside the prison.

There was a sound at the door. Proteus turned as Dymas hurried into the cell.

"Proteus, come quickly," said his father.

"What—?"

Dymas took Proteus's arm. "There's a ship waiting in the harbor. A crew of my most trusted officers will take you far from Syracuse," he whispered.

"But—the ambassadors' guards," objected Proteus.

". . . Are asleep or well bribed. But we must go now."

"Go where? To live the rest of my life in exile?"

"To *live*, son," said Dymas. "I won't let them execute you for Sinbad's crime."

"Neither will Sinbad," Proteus replied.

"Proteus. . . don't be foolish. Sinbad has no intention of going to Tartarus. The Sinbad you knew as a child—"

Proteus cut him off. "—is still in him as a man. I've seen it."

"Proteus—" pleaded his father.

Proteus looked away and then put his hands on Dymas's shoulders. "Go, Father," he said gently. "I know what I am doing."

Dymas bowed his head. Then he turned and left the cell.

Proteus went again to the window, looking out at the moon. But now a hint of doubt shadowed his face.

The next day found the *Chimera* moored off an unusually shaped island. Its spiky ridges climbed precipitously to the sky, and it was covered in a strange purple and green vegetation. No one on the crew had ever seen such odd-looking plants before.

"We're here for ten minutes," Kale was warning the crew. "If you get lost, you'll get left behind."

DMeanwhile, Sinbad stood on the top deck with Spike, surveying his ship. He was in an absolute dither. "Can you believe . . . Over here . . . And here . . . I—I just don't . . . How did one woman *do* so much damage?" He seemed to have forgotten the treachery of the Dragon's Teeth and the miracle that they'd made it through.

A piece of the railing broke off in his hand, and Sinbad grimaced. He walked up to Kale, sighing as he gave orders. "All right, I'm gonna need the full set of chisels, the jackplane, and about a cord of cut wood."

Kale shouted to the crew, relaying the orders. "All right, men—you heard the captain! Find some logs and be quick about it!" The crew hustled down the gangplank onto the beach while, groaning under his breath, Sinbad looked closely at the damage.

Marina walked past Sinbad and stopped. "Oh, for heaven's sake," she said. "You only need a little tree sap and she'll be as good as new."

"When I want your advice, I'll give it to you." Sinbad turned to see that Marina had already grabbed a bucket from the deck, and was striding down the gangplank.

"Hey—hey—hey—where do ya think you're goin'?" Sinbad called after her.

Marina ignored him. Spike, tail wagging, followed her down the gangplank.

"Well, fine," said Sinbad. "At least take someone with you—" He was immediately drowned out by a loud chorus from the crew, rushing to offer all kinds of assistance to Marina.

Rat and Li helped her step off the gangplank. "Right this way, *signorina*," said Rat.

"May I assist you, lady?" said Li. In Cantonese, he added, "Mind the steps. I'll show you the way."

"Why, thank you," said Marina, with a significant glance back at Sinbad. "How nice to see *some* men haven't forgotten common courtesy."

Spike bounded over to Marina's side. Sinbad shook his head in disgust, and sighed heavily. She sure had them all wrapped around her finger—even Spike, he thought.

Kale started down the ramp to join the stampede to help Marina. "Not so fast," said Sinbad, stopping him.

"But you know, she's right, tree sap would be perfect for—"

Sinbad cut him off. "Just—just stay with the ship," he said. Then he jumped over the rail and stomped off after Marina himself.

He caught up with her as she trooped across the island with the other crew members. "I already said thank you," he said grumpily. "That's what this is all about, isn't it?"

Marina approached a large tree and inspected the trunk. "It's about repairing the ship. If I break something, I fix it." She stuck her hand out without looking at him. "Um, knife please."

"Oh, yeah—like I'd give you a weapon."

In a flash, the other men produced an array of deadly blades, each eagerly offering a weapon to Marina. Pleased, she made her selection. "Thank you, Rat," she said sweetly.

She smiled at Sinbad, who walked toward her, passing Rat. "You really ought to be more courteous —" Rat began to tell him helpfully, but his advice was cut short by Sinbad's fist connecting with his jaw.

Sinbad didn't even look back as Rat hit the ground. He just kept walking. "Oh, great!" he muttered sourly. "Now I'm getting etiquette lessons from a bilge rat!"

"Well, she did save the ship, Captain," Luca pointed out.

Marina smiled graciously. "Why, thank you, Luca," she said.

As Marina sliced into the tree trunk, the top of the tree suddenly retracted. Marina drew back a little, startled, but then decided she'd imagined it. She continued her work, holding the bucket below the cut to catch the sap.

Meanwhile, in the background, the crew had clustered around Sinbad, continuing to sing Marina's praises.

". . . And now she's helping to fix it," Rat was pointing out, holding his swollen jaw.

"Very handy, I say," Jin agreed.

"And brave," Li chimed in.

"This girl," said Sinbad irritably, "wouldn't know how to fix a broken fingernail."

Marina walked up to him, carrying a full bucket of sap. "Honestly," she said, "you are the most boorish, pigheaded man I've ever met!"

"Hey, lady," Sinbad replied, turning his back on her

and walking away, "I've seen the highborn boys your type hangs out with. And I'm the only man you've ever met!" Shoulders bunched, head forward, he started to march back to the ship, satisfied about having put Marina in her place.

WHAM! The bucket of tree sap hit him in the back of the head and slopped all over him.

"Whoa," said Rat. The crew grimaced, but secretly, of course, they were loving this, and eager to see how Sinbad would react.

Slowly, Sinbad turned and looked at Marina. Marina, hands on hips, stared back.

Very deliberately, Sinbad picked up an enormous handful of glop.

"Oh no," said Marina, backing away. "Oh ho ho, no no no— No!"

SPLOOSH! She got it right in the face.

Jin stuck his hand out to Li. "Five on Marina," he said.

Marina slapped muck off her face, moving in on Sinbad. "You egotistical, selfish—"

Sinbad held his ground. "You spoiled—"

"Disrespectful—" she continued. She picked up something without even looking at it, some sort of a large, crablike creature. "Pretentious—" she went on.

"Deluded—" he said.

She lobbed the giant crab-thing at Sinbad's head in

midinsult. "Pompous—" she added as Sinbad dodged. "Self-centered—"

Sinbad started toward her. "High-and-mighty—" he added to his list.

BOP! She nailed him in the jaw with a clump of dirt. He shook it off and kept moving in on her.

Marina was really on a roll now: "Untrustworthy, ungrateful, impossible, insufferable—"

Sinbad was now right in her face. "At least I'm not repressed!" he yelled at her.

"Repressed?" she yelled right back at him, struggling to pick up a huge rock to throw. "I'll show you repressed!" With a mighty effort, she pulled it loose and heaved it up over her head.

All at once, the island was rocked by tremors. A flock of birds rose in a cloud and took flight off a mountain in the distance. Something was terribly wrong.

Marina and Sinbad both looked at the rock Marina was still holding. "Put it back," Sinbad said quietly.

Marina laughed nervously in the sudden stillness.

And then, behind them, a gigantic fishtail arose out of the water. Marina stared, wide-eyed. The mountain was now making a strange gurgling sound.

Slowly, a gigantic eye opened beneath their feet, its lids retracting to reveal its full size. It was as big as a skating pond, and almost as slippery.

Rat fell with a splat into the eyeball and struggled to

pull himself free from the ooze. "Eeeeewwwww," he cried.

Spike took a little slurp of the goo on the surface. He spat it out with a *bleeagh*.

"Run!" yelled Sinbad suddenly.

They all broke into a run, as the enormous fish on which they had been standing was fully revealed. Its head was spiky, its teeth were as big as oak trees, and it was not happy.

"Come on!" Sinbad shouted.

They all dashed back to the ship, running for their lives as the fish started to dive into the water. "*O Dio mio, un pesce gigante!*" Rat was yelling. "Oh my God, a giant fish!"

"It's alive! It's alive! The island is alive!" Jin screamed.

"The island is a fish! The island is a giant fish!" Li added in Chinese.

On the ship, Kale looked up from his repair work, surprised at the commotion. "Kale!" Sinbad shouted from the distance. "Kale!" Suddenly, the entire deck jolted beneath him, and a towering fin surged upward from the water, casting the entire ship into shadow.

"What? Whoa . . ." was all Kale could get out.

Meanwhile, back on the island-fish, Sinbad, Marina, and the crew were bolting down a slope toward the ship when the ground opened up beneath them. Water gushed out of the newly formed chasm, blocking their path. It was the creature's massive gill.

The fish was submerging, and there was no time to waste. Sinbad grabbed Marina by the wrist and leaped through the venting water that spewed up from the gill. "Jump!" he yelled. They made it past the gill, landing safely on a slippery fin, but barely had time to recover their balance before the entire crew came crashing through the spouting water. The whole group became a slipping, sliding, out-of-control mess of limbs as they careened down the fin and flew into midair toward the boat.

The whole bunch of them slammed into the rigging, barely catching themselves. Sinbad, holding on to Marina, caught a rope and swung onto the top deck.

"Veer off, Kale!" Sinbad yelled before his feet had even touched the deck.

"The star!" Marina reminded Kale.

"Hold your heading!" Sinbad added. Without losing a second, Sinbad leaped to the front of the boat, scooping up a rope and hook as he went. He threw the loose end to Rat.

"Rat! Tie this off!" he shouted.

Rat was too dazed to respond. "Wh-what?" he said.

Without waiting, Sinbad scrambled to the front of the ship and heaved the hook toward the moving island-fish. It clanged along the creature's side, and then lodged between its rocky scales.

"Ha!" Sinbad cried in triumph.

"Wait!" yelled Rat. The rope snapped tight, and Sinbad was thrown face first to the deck as the *Chimera* rocketed forward. The fish was towing the ship in its wake.

"Yee-haaah!" whooped Sinbad at the prow. His plan had worked.

The ship made incredible progress, up one towering swell and down again with a crash, and then up another and down again, *crash*, and another. . . and another . . . and another . . .

Quite a while later, Sinbad was doubled over, holding on to the side of the ship. Kale staggered toward him. "Sinbad," he said, "the men can't take much more."

"I can't take much more either," said Sinbad, as green as one of the ship's pickles. "Cut the line."

Thunk! Kale's sword cut the rope and the *Chimera* instantly slowed.

Along the sides of the ship, the crew members hung over the rails, struggling to keep down their last meals. Spike ran up to a group of them. He didn't look too good.

They scrambled to get out of the way. "No! No! No!" they yelled, but it was too late. Spike lost his lunch all over the deck. "Spiiike!" they wailed.

"Hey, where'd he get the carrots?" Jed wondered.

Sinbad lurched over to a bulkhead and slumped

down. Nearby, he spotted a sick-looking Marina, standing at the rail. "Whose idea was that again?" he said to her.

Marina stumbled over and sat down next to him. "I don't know," she replied, "but he owes me lunch."

The two of them sat together for a while in comfortable silence, until they realized they were feeling a little too comfortable for comfort. Marina belonged to Proteus; they both knew it. But what, then, was this electricity they kept feeling between them?

Finally, their attention was attracted by the spectacular view and the towering stone they were approaching. It gave them an excuse to break the moment.

CHAPTER NINE

*T*he *Chimera* sailed underneath the rough stone gates, which looked as if they had been thrown down from the heavens eons ago by a careless god. They formed a portal: two massive pillars and a crosspiece slapped on top to connect them. The gateway was so tall that the *Chimera* was like a miniature toy beneath it.

"The Granite Gates," said Sinbad, craning his neck upward in wonderment. "Bet you never thought I'd get us this far."

"No, I didn't, but Proteus did. For some reason, he trusts you," said Marina, with a look in her eye that showed she was beginning to believe in Sinbad, too.

"What could he have been thinking?" Sinbad said with a wry smile.

"How did you two ever meet?" she asked.

"Running for my life, as usual," Sinbad answered. He watched Marina for a moment, guarded. After a moment's consideration, he decided to continue. "A couple of angry thugs had cornered me outside the palace walls. I was trapped. A sword at my throat, at my chest, at my. . . well, you get the idea. And then suddenly, there was a fourth blade. Proteus had watched it all from his room in the palace. He had actually climbed down the castle wall to fight at my side. And boy, did we fight. It was like we'd rehearsed it. We were best friends from that day forward."

"What happened with you two?" she asked gently.

Sinbad's reverie was broken. He looked suddenly uncomfortable. "We took different paths," he said, and abruptly turned away.

Marina stared after him, a bit shocked and more than a bit curious.

Up in Tartarus, Eris was taking a bath, a bubble bath. But as always, she was watching. Soaking in her strange, murky, celestial pool, she regarded Marina through a perfect, iridescent bubble that was balanced on her well-manicured finger. In fact, there were thousands of bubbles, and she could see Marina in all of them.

"Enough talking," she said. "Time for some screaming."

She blew on the bubble and it froze, dropping into her hand. She shook it like a snow globe. Then she crushed it in her fist.

When she opened her palm, a strange, bird-shaped ice form had replaced it. She smiled wickedly. Leaning back in her bath, she blew on the bird, sending it flying off.

The *Chimera* was becoming trapped in a frozen sea. Stunned and frustrated, Sinbad climbed to the top deck as a blizzard howled around him.

"Oh, for crying out loud," he moaned to himself. "What next?"

He walked past Kale. "Get a shirt on," he said, glancing at Kale's huge bare chest.

Leaping down to the frozen surface, the crew formed a line in front of the boat, cutting and chopping a path through the ice for the ship. Rat and Kale were foremost among them.

"Steal the Book of Peace!" Rat grumbled with each swing of the pick. Sinbad had certainly not promised ice. "We'll retire in the tropics," he muttered bitterly.

On the deck, Spike heard something, pricked up his ears, and barked. Sinbad stopped to look at him.

A strange sound echoed across the ice. Sinbad turned, listening. It was getting louder, reverberating across the still snowscape.

As Spike continued to bark, the ship's crew stopped working to see what was happening. Marina looked around, too, and Spike jumped up near her. He was extremely agitated.

Then Marina saw something flying above the cliffs in the distance. It was getting closer, then disappearing again behind the ice. With a yelp, Spike bolted toward the stern.

And then it happened. Crashing over the snowy cliff, a gigantic, terrifying bird of prey with lethal talons swooped down at Marina. It was the infamous Roc, fabled terror of all sailors, looking for prey.

Shrieking, it dove toward the *Chimera* as Marina crouched down on the deck. At the stern, Sinbad ducked as the Roc soared over his head. Leaping to his feet, Sinbad shouted a warning to his crew on the ice: "Everyone back on the ship!"

Yelling, the sailors raced across the ice for the ship. "Come on! Come on!" Kale urged them.

"Hurry!" Marina shouted.

The Roc circled and then dove straight for the men, aiming for Jed, the last sailor on the ice. Just as the Roc's sharp talons were about to close on him, Jed jumped into the icy water.

The Roc circled the ship again, looking for a victim. Marina looked over the side to see Jed surface, gasping for air and fumbling for a hold on the ice. "Jed! Grab the rope!" she yelled, throwing one overboard to him.

Sinbad hauled Kale on board, just in time to see

the Roc swooping down toward the boat again.

"Rat! Give me your hand!" Kale shouted.

Glancing over to where Marina was helping Jed, Sinbad saw that the Roc was heading straight for her. "Marina!" he gasped. He raced across the deck. Marina turned and tried to run, but the Roc was right behind her. It reached one mighty talon forward and snatched her up.

Sinbad lunged toward Marina, managed to grab her hand, and was dragged across the deck as the bird flew upward. But the Roc's hold was too strong. It pulled Marina out of Sinbad's grasp. He watched helplessly as Marina was carried away.

The Roc streaked up, up, up, until it had reached its nearby aerie. The nest sat at the top of a high, forbidding ice tower, a deeply carved path spiraling up to the pinnacle. The bird dropped Marina into its lair and landed beside her. Shrieking, it turned toward her. Marina tried to run, but the Roc's giant, clawed foot came down over her. She squirmed desperately. Although her jacket was caught fast, she wriggled free. The giant bird stabbed down with its beak and then lifted its head in fury, shaking Marina's empty coat and tossing it aside.

Again it slammed its talons down, but Marina was already on the run, darting behind the Roc, looking for somewhere to hide. She dove under a giant rib cage, obviously the remains of some previous meal—not a good sign for her future.

Screeching, the Roc turned and searched for Marina. She shrank back against the cage of bones, desperately trying to avoid the bird's sight.

Back on the deck of the *Chimera*, Sinbad was busy tying sharp spikes onto his boots. "Hey, Rat! Keep the blocks from seizing!" he yelled. All they needed now was for the equipment to freeze up.

"Aye, aye, Captain!"

"And Kale!" said Sinbad.

"Aye."

"Gimme a hug," Sinbad said. He spread his arms wide, ignoring Kale's befuddled look.

"Excuse me?" said Kale, backing away in shock as Sinbad started toward him. He grimaced as Sinbad wrapped his arms around him.

In a flash, Sinbad pulled the two daggers from the sheaths on Kale's back. Grinning, he stepped back, brandishing the daggers.

"Hmmm," said Kale as he started to understand what Sinbad had in mind.

With his foot, Sinbad flipped a shield up into his hands and deftly strapped it to his back. Then he turned and ran toward the prow, with Spike bounding after him. At the prow, Sinbad aimed a huge crossbow at the icy tower, and took a deep breath. He whistled to Spike, who pulled the bone-handled lever that released the crossbow. The harpoon, laden with ice, shot up and out.

A dagger between his teeth, Sinbad grabbed hold of the rope that was attached to the harpoon and was pulled into the air toward the ice wall. Kale and the crew watched in amazement as their captain flew through the air.

As the spear hit the massive block of ice, Sinbad released the rope and went into a free fall toward the ice wall, stabbing into the ice with the spikes on both feet and the daggers in his hands.

It was a hard landing. Sinbad turned and spat out a mouthful of snow. Far below him, the *Chimera* waited as he started the long climb up the ice wall.

"She couldn't see the bird? Everyone else saw it—it's as big as the friggin' ship, how could you not see it?" he groused to himself as he climbed. "But Marina? Marina's looking the other way . . . "

A freezing Marina peeked around her bony cage to see where the Roc was. Suddenly, behind her, a gloved hand covered her mouth, muffling her surprised shout. At the other side of the aerie, the Roc turned its head and shrieked at the small sound.

Hidden behind the wall of snow and ice, Sinbad kept

Marina's mouth covered with his hand. "Shhh!" he said fiercely. He turned to keep his eyes on the Roc, who was not far off.

Marina pushed his hand away. "You're rescuing me!" she whispered joyfully.

"Yes, if that's what you want to call it. But this is gonna cost you another diamond. Rescues aren't part of the usual tourist package."

"So—how are we gonna get down?" she whispered.

Sinbad studied the situation. "I—I don't know yet . . ." he admitted.

"*What?*" she responded in an angry whisper.

Sinbad clamped his hand over her mouth again. "Well, I'm thinking about it," he said defensively. "I'm thinking about it, all right?"

Marina pulled his hand away—again. "You scaled a thousand-foot tower of ice and you don't know how to get down?"

"Of all the ungrateful—" sputtered Sinbad, flustered. "Look, if you'd rather take your chances on your own, that can be arranged."

They could hear the Roc getting closer. This time Marina clamped her hand over Sinbad's mouth. "Shh-shh-shh," she went. "All right, all right. What do we have to work with? Umm . . . Ropes?" she whispered, trying to be helpful.

Sinbad looked at her sheepishly. "No."

"Grappling hooks?"

"Yeah . . . no," he corrected himself, under his breath.

Marina was pleading for good news now. "Your swords?"

"Ahhg," he replied. He dug around and pulled out one of Kale's daggers. The other had been lost on his crash landing. "Hey—I've got this!" he said.

"Great," Marina shot back. "He can pick his teeth when he's done with us."

"Yeah. Okay, see, in the hands of an expert, a good knife has a thousand and one uses," Sinbad retorted. He spun the dagger and flipped it, demonstrating his prowess. It hit the ice above them, and with a crash, their hiding place collapsed around them.

The Roc heard the commotion, turned, and looked right at them. Wordlessly, Marina smacked Sinbad.

Shrieking, the Roc charged toward them. Sinbad grabbed Marina and pulled her away. "Come on!" he said. They ran.

Suddenly, Marina realized that they were right at the towering cliff's edge. "What—?" she said, hesitating.

But there was no time. Sinbad yanked her right over the edge. "Let's gooooooo!" he yelled, his voice echoing down the ice chasm.

"NOOOOOOOOO!!!" she yelled as she plummeted.

They fell and fell and fell. As they plunged, Sinbad frantically manipulated the shield underneath him. He pulled Marina on top with him, and they slammed down onto the side of the tower. The shield-sled flew down the slope like a shot.

Instantly, they became an out-of-control tangle of limbs. Each of them grappled separately to gain purchase on the careening shield.

"Would you—your elbow! Watch that!" Sinbad yelped. "Ow! Just get your foot off—"

"Whoa! I need to—" Marina grunted, struggling to get a better position. "I can't see anything, and what—ugh—watch your dagger!"

They twisted and turned down the outside of the tower, hurtling down the spiral path lined with imposing columns. Through the openings between the columns, far below, they could see the waiting *Chimera*. "I think we lost him," Sinbad said to Marina, panting.

As if in answer, the shrieking Roc swooped down and landed directly in their path.

"I don't think so," yelled Marina.

Now the huge, angry-looking bird began zooming in at them, over and over, slamming into the ice and rock as he tried to snatch them up in his curved, razorlike beak. On the last attack, Sinbad whipped the shield out from beneath them and used it to fend off the Roc. A jet of snow and ice shot up Sinbad's coat as he slid. "Wh-who-whoooh." He shuddered, shocked by the cold. Shrieking loudly, the Roc swooped away. Sinbad quickly flipped back onto the shield, pulling Marina along with him.

As the Roc wheeled to begin another attack, it struck a precarious column along the path, sending it toppling into the next one. Suddenly, like a giant set of dominoes, the columns started to topple, coming down all around Sinbad and Marina. They found themselves dodging and weaving between collapsing stone pillars that were the size of small houses. The pillars shook the whole tower as they fell.

"Corner!" Sinbad shouted to Marina. "Hard left—your other left! Port! Port! Port!"

Turning, he glimpsed an opening between the columns, in the side of the tower. "Lean right!" he ordered. Grabbing Marina, Sinbad pulled her hard to the right.

"AAAAHHH!" Marina screamed as the Roc's huge talons crashed into the snow, barely missing them.

They were skidding toward the narrow openings in the tower, Marina almost flying off the shield. Sinbad had only a tenuous hold on her.

"Sinbad! No!" she shrieked as she saw the tiny space between the columns that they were going to have to shoot through.

Sinbad pulled her up on her feet and she flung her arms around him. Using the shield as a snowboard now, they barely squeezed between the columns and into the tower.

Standing on the shield as it flew through the inside of the tower, Marina looked down. "Whoa!" she yelled in terror.

They ground to a stop at the edge of a huge precipice. Although they were still facing dire consequences, Sinbad was quite pleased with himself at their success so far.

As they caught their breath, they failed to notice a shadow growing larger and larger on the ice wall behind them. Suddenly, the Roc crashed through the ice wall and came straight for them.

. . . And they were off again. They ran screaming through the tower, the Roc just a few feet behind them. Just as it was about to catch up with them, Sinbad spotted a shaft of sunlight shining through an opening. "Hang on!" he yelled. Planting his dagger as hard as he could in the ice, he used it to swing them around toward the opening. They flew out of the tower in a cloud of snow and ice, the shield spinning through the air.

The *Chimera* crew looked up, not surprised at all by their return. "Yep—there they are," said Kale casually.

Yelling and screaming, Marina and Sinbad plummeted down toward the *Chimera* far below. In the nick of time, they broke their fall against a sail and tumbled down onto the deck, bringing the sail down on top of them.

They lay wrapped in the canvas, a jumble of limbs

tangled every which way. Sitting back slowly, Sinbad looked down at Marina. "There," he said. "Just as I— planned." She looked up at him. And she laughed. Sinbad smiled back at her, relieved that she wasn't mad.

Then the sail was pulled back and the entire *Chimera* crew surrounded them.

"It's Marina!" they shouted, dancing around in ecstasy. They were all smiles as they helped her to her feet.

"Wow! I can't believe you came back." Li grinned, not caring that no one could understand his Cantonese. "It really is unbelievable. We should celebrate. How about a feast or something?"

Overcome with emotion, Rat collapsed, hugging Marina around the waist. "We thought you were gone . . . forever!" he sobbed.

Sinbad was slowly getting to his feet. No one was paying any attention to him at all. "Oh, I'm fine. Really," he said, holding up his hand in mock protest. "But I'm touched by your concern." He put his hands on his back, grimacing in exaggerated pain. His back made a cracking noise.

From behind him, there was another, louder *crack*. Then a deep rumble. And then . . . *CRASH!* Mystified, Sinbad turned to see the remaining columns of the Roc's tower falling like dominoes: *CRASH! CRASH! CRASH!*

As the last column fell, it hit the ice field that lay

before the *Chimera*, shattering it—and opening a wide waterway through the ice, to the open ocean beyond. Sinbad, Marina, and the crew exchanged looks that quickly turned to smiles, and then cheers. The *Chimera* was set free and the Roc was nowhere to be found.

Grinning, Sinbad turned to Marina, who gave him a warm look.

CHAPTER TEN

The *Chimera* sailed swiftly through the night, still following Eris's star.

Marina walked around the deck, looking out at the ocean. It was a beautiful night. When she spotted Sinbad at the wheel, she made her way to him.

"Sinbad . . . thank you for coming after me," she said hesitantly.

He turned, smiled, and surprised himself by replying with a simple and sincere "You're welcome." He turned away again. She watched him for a moment. Something had clearly changed in their relationship, and they both felt it. It didn't feel like a game anymore.

"This life suits you," she observed.

"I wasn't made for dry land," he replied. He turned to her again. "And you? Is it the shore or the sea?"

She walked toward him. "I've always loved the sea— even dreamed of a life on it. But it wasn't meant to be. I have responsibilities in Syracuse."

"You really have to give it up?" Sinbad had to admit that she was an able seawoman. They wouldn't have made it this far had she not been on board.

"Yes," she said. She looked over the ocean.

Sinbad looked at her for a moment, and then placed his hand on hers. Surprised, Marina turned to him. He smiled and guided her to the helm, put her hand on the wheel, and stepped back. They smiled at each other. She was steering the ship.

"You know," Sinbad said, "I've traveled the world. Seen things no other man has seen . . ." They stood close together, looking out over the dark waves. "But nothing . . . nothing compares to the open sea," he said.

Marina was touched by his honest words. "And is this what you always wanted?" she asked him.

Sinbad smiled gently. "Not really," he replied. "When we were young, Proteus and I used to talk about joining the Royal Navy and serving Syracuse side by side. But as we got older, our lives began to change. He's a prince and I'm—well . . ." He could not bring himself to finish the sentence. "I was never jealous of him, though, until one morning a ship came into harbor. A ship with his future on it. It was the most beautiful thing I'd ever seen."

Marina smiled. "What was on the ship?" she asked in a soft voice.

Sinbad turned to her. "You," he said.

She looked at him, utterly stunned.

"Proteus met you at the dock," he explained. "I jumped on the first outbound ship and never looked back." He looked at her, into her eyes, their faces very close. "Until now," he added finally.

Marina gazed at him, deeply moved. They were drawn closer together, and Sinbad took her hand. They were almost close enough to kiss. But they both stopped.

A crash of thunder startled them. Then a flash of light cut through the darkness before them. A shooting star. They smiled.

Then there was another flash. Their smiles faded as they realized that something wasn't right.

"The gates of Tartarus," whispered Sinbad, full of dread.

Then a cascade of shooting stars streaked across the sky toward Eris's star, which now hung directly in their path.

Sinbad and Marina looked at each other. It was time.

The crew knew it, too. Spike came dashing up through the hatch to join them on the deck, followed immediately by Kale.

Soon all hands were on deck. Standing with Sinbad and Marina, the crew gazed in amazement at what lay before them.

Eris's star was really a colossal gateway, floating in the night sky before them.

Marina and Sinbad looked down into the water, which appeared tattered, as if they were floating over a vast galaxy of stars.

"Rat! Give me a lookout!" Sinbad shouted up to his rigger.

Rat scurried up to the crow's nest and peered into the distance. He blinked. He looked again, to make sure he was really seeing it:

The end of the Earth.

And out past where the ocean dropped off a steep edge, beyond that, lay Eris's star, the gateway to Tartarus. "Oh," he said softly. "We're dead."

"What is it?" Sinbad called from below.

"It just ends, Captain!" Rat reported. "It's the edge of the world!"

Jin held his hand out to Li. "Pay up," he said. "It's flat."

Luca was ready to throw in the towel. "That's it! Time to go home," he announced.

Kale's huge hand closed on Luca's shoulder, stopping him in his tracks. "The captain hasn't given his orders yet."

Everyone looked to Sinbad, who was staring ahead intently. "Follow that star beyond the horizon," he said to himself.

Ahead of them was a tall, rocky island, divided by a strange, glowing cleft. As Sinbad looked at it, he realized that it was surrounded by a powerful updraft. Standing at the wheel, he watched it for a while, and then looked up at his sails. Marina watched him closely.

"Sinbad?" she said, concerned.

Suddenly, he sprang into action, leaping down to the deck. "Men! All hands to your posts!" he shouted. "Free all sheets and wait for my command."

The men stared at him. Was he crazy? Undo the ropes that held the sails?

Sinbad hurried down the deck, shouting at them to get moving: "Now! Go! Go! Go!"

The men scattered and got to work, but Kale moved to intercept Sinbad. "Sinbad. How are we going to—"

"Just trust me!" Sinbad said, cutting him off.

Now Sinbad shouted up to the crow's nest. "Rat! Rig the main yard to the fo'c'sle!"

"But that would stop us dead!" Rat shouted back.

"Just do it!"

"Aye, aye, Cap'n."

Rat scurried out across the yardarm, lost his balance and fell underneath, grabbed a line, and swung wildly across to another mast.

As he watched Rat's acrobatics, Sinbad shouted orders to the crew. "Slack to all sheets!" he yelled.

"Aye, Cap'n!" Luca responded.

"Cut the fore and main trusses! Move! Move! Move!

Aft yard astern!" Sinbad commanded.

The crew hurried to follow his orders and tried to figure out his master plan. "But that's—" Jed protested.

Sinbad cut him off. "Crazy, I know. Now hurry! Swing the fo'c'sle to port! Ease the aft! Full hoist to forward sails!"

"Aye, aye, Captain!" said a female voice. Surprised, Sinbad stopped and saw Marina pitching in to follow orders. He smiled and then went back to shouting commands.

"*Pull!*" he ordered everyone.

The crew strained at the ropes. The sails billowed out. The *Chimera* sailed closer and closer to the edge. "Tie off all sails!" Sinbad yelled. "All hands amidships— and pray to the gods!" More to himself, he added, a bit warily: "We may be meeting them soon."

Sinbad stood at the bow next to Marina and Spike. They were now right at the edge.

"We're going to die!" shrieked Rat, ducking down into the crow's nest.

They all braced themselves. The prow went over.

The *Chimera* tipped over the edge. It fell.

Everyone screamed as the ship dropped for a horrifying moment, then dropped farther still. "Come on, come on, come on . . ." Sinbad pleaded under his breath.

Then, like parachutes opening, the sails filled in the updraft, and the ship was lifted up. They were flying.

Everyone gasped and looked around. They were still alive! A huge cheer went up.

"It worked!" Sinbad said in disbelief, both to Marina and himself.

"Sinbad, you did it!" cried Kale.

Accompanied by the sound of the crew cheering, the *Chimera* flew out across the abyss toward the floating stone arch that surrounded the glowing entrance to Tartarus. It looked like a huge mouth grinning at them.

Sinbad studied it briefly, and hastily decided on his plan. As the ship soared toward the gaping arch, Sinbad stood with one foot up on the rail. "Hard over to port, Grum!" he ordered.

Sinbad tied off a rope and then turned to Marina and his crew. They were all watching him now.

"Kale!" said Sinbad.

Solemnly, Kale stepped forward. "Aye!" he said snappily.

"If I don't make it, the ship is yours," Sinbad told him. Then he saluted the crew. "Gentlemen," he said, "it's been a privilege robbing with you."

Marina stepped forward. "I'm coming with you," she said, in a voice that told Sinbad she was serious.

Sinbad started to say something, but Marina interrupted. "And don't tell me the realm of Chaos is no place for a woman," she reminded him.

Without a word, Sinbad pulled Marina to him. He

wrapped the rope around her waist, and then around himself, pulling her even closer. "I would never say that," he whispered.

Marina smiled at him, and then they jumped over the rail.

The crew looked over the side as Marina and Sinbad swung down and under the airborne *Chimera*. With Spike behind them, they all rushed to the other side just in time to see them swing toward the arch—and then through it. Then they disappeared.

As the crew quickly prepared to steer the ship back toward the safety of the ocean, the empty rope swung back toward the *Chimera*.

Sinbad and Marina were gone.

CHAPTER ELEVEN

S uddenly Sinbad and Marina were not falling. They were just standing amid the bleak world of Tartarus, a swirling wasteland of sand. The dunes shifted and writhed, revealing the wreckage of civilizations come and gone, great armies marching to oblivion, and skeletal heroes on noble quests long forgotten. Suddenly, a wicked menagerie of celestial monsters appeared, surrounding Sinbad and Marina. The creatures edged closer to them.

They heard Eris's voice, wafting toward them from the ebony shadows and swirling images. "Now, now, my pets," they heard her say. "Is this any way to treat a guest?"

Like a parting tide, the sands of Tartarus flowed away, revealing a pair of facing chairs, their neat informality out of place in the vast sweep of Eris's realm.

"Okay, I'm severely creeped out," Sinbad said into Marina's ear.

And then, Eris appeared in all her imperious and playful glory. "Bravo," she said. "No mortal has ever made it to Tartarus before. Alive, that is. Make yourself at home."

"Nice place you've got here," Sinbad responded.

"Like it?" said the goddess. "I'm planning on doing the whole world this way."

"Wow," he said, "good plan. You sound busy, so listen, we'll just take the Book of Peace and get out of your way."

"What makes you think I have it?"

"You framed me for the theft," he told her. "So they would execute me."

"You . . . ?" said Eris, one eyebrow raised.

Suddenly, the truth dawned on Sinbad. "No," he cried, "Proteus! You knew he would take my place!"

"What a clever little man you are."

"You thought I'd run," said Sinbad. "Then Proteus would die and Syracuse would be—"

"Left without the next rightful king, and tumble into glorious chaos," she said with a sigh. "You humans are so predictable. Proteus couldn't help being ever so noble and you couldn't help betraying him."

With a rumbling sound, a familiar figure approached them from above. It was Cetus, healthy and surly as ever.

"But I didn't betray Proteus!" Sinbad protested. "I didn't run away."

"Oh, but you did betray him. You stole his only love! He's not even in his grave yet and you're moving in on his girl! Face it, your heart is as black as mine."

Marina stepped forward. "You don't know what's in his heart," she said.

"Oh yes I do," Eris countered. "And more importantly, so does he." She turned to Sinbad. "In your heart you know that Proteus is going to die because he saw something in you that just isn't there," she told him.

"No!" he cried. She was wrong . . . wasn't she?

"Wanna bet?" she said with a wicked smile. "I'll tell you what. Let's play a game, and if you win, I'll give you the Book of Peace."

Eris waved her hand and the Book of Peace appeared on a floating platform. "There it is, noble hero," she said.

He began to climb the floating steps that approached the platform, but the first one crumbled beneath his foot.

"Not so fast," Eris said. "My game has rules, Sinbad. I'll ask you a question. One simple question. If you answer truthfully, the Book is yours."

Sinbad looked at her, suspicious. "Give me your word," he said.

Eris sighed. "You still don't trust me?" she said, looking sweet and innocent.

"Ah . . . no," said Sinbad. That one was a no-brainer.

"Isn't it a pity we live in such skeptical times?" she said. "Oh, all right, you have my word as a goddess!"

Eris crossed her heart to show her sincerity, but the gesture became frightening and demonic as the X burned into her chest with a fiery light. It was a hugely magnified echo of what he'd seen in their encounter under the sea. "Fair enough?" she challenged.

Sinbad focused on the Book, preparing himself, his eyes blazing. "Ask your question," he said.

"Excellent. Now we all know what happens if you get the Book of Peace: you return it to Syracuse and save Proteus. But here's my question, Sinbad . . ."

She loomed up behind Sinbad in menacing anticipation, letting a long moment pass before she finished:

"If you don't get the Book, will you sail for the horizon with the love you stole from him, or will you go back to die in his place?"

Sinbad looked at Marina, then at the Book. And then back to Eris.

"I will go back," he said at last.

Nothing moved.

Tartarus echoed eerily as Sinbad took his first step across the fragile platform. Uncertain at first, he gained confidence until, finally, he was within reach of the Book.

Then the cracks appeared, growing like a spiderweb beneath him.

"You're lying," Eris declared.

Instantly, the ground beneath Sinbad shattered violently. Only inches from the Book, he dropped away, making one final, futile grab for the prize.

But before his hand could grasp its ancient pages, Sinbad and Marina were hurled out of Tartarus with the sound of Eris's mocking laughter echoing in their ears. The arch slammed shut behind them.

It was lost, all lost. Now only disaster and chaos awaited. Eris had won.

CHAPTER TWELVE

Sinbad and Marina found themselves sitting side by side on a sandbar jutting out from a barren island. Gray waves swept the shore. They felt utterly defeated.

The gateway to Tartarus, now inert and lifeless, hung in the distance.

Marina glanced at Sinbad. He was silent. It was over. The quest had failed.

"I'm sorry," Sinbad said at last. "Eris is right about me."

"No, she's not. You answered her question. You told the truth." Marina was surprised at the words coming out of her own mouth. Just a short while before, she would never have imagined herself trying to convince Sinbad that he had a noble side.

"It wasn't the truth. It was me, trying to pass myself off as someone I'm not."

"Sinbad, I've seen who you are. You don't need to pretend. Eris trapped you. Why should you or Proteus or anyone have to die?"

"Marina —" he began hopelessly.

She sprang to her feet, full of desperate emotion. "No!" she cried. "You need to escape. Get as far away as you can. I'll go back. I'll explain everything."

"No, Marina."

"I can't watch you die—" She stopped, tears streaming down her face. "I love you."

A long moment passed as Marina's words hung in the air, their impact hitting him with full force.

Sinbad was stunned at first. Then he found himself overcome with a sense of clarity and resolve he had never encountered in his lifetime of trickery.

"But could you love a man who would run away?" he asked, moving to her side.

They embraced, while behind them, the *Chimera* approached.

The sun was setting on the dark and ruined city of Syracuse. King Dymas approached Proteus in his cell. They hugged one last time, and then the doors opened.

As Dymas watched, Proteus was marched out of the prison. The king bowed his head. Across the grand courtyard, Proteus walked toward the execution block.

All around the harbor, the people of Syracuse had

gathered. Only the sounds of a bell tolling and the lapping water in the harbor broke the desolate silence.

At the steps to the platform, Proteus stopped. Two women drew his shirt back from his shoulders and exposed his regal neck. Proteus looked out at the horizon once more. Finally, he accepted the truth. Sinbad would not come in time.

Proteus knelt, placing his head on the block. As the axe was raised, Dymas turned away.

Suddenly, a sword came spinning through the air, slicing the axe handle in half. The blade landed inches from Proteus's head, and the metal surface reflected his astonished face.

Proteus caught his breath and looked up to see Sinbad walking toward him.

Meanwhile, the crew of the *Chimera* were scaling the wall behind Sinbad to reach the platform. Proteus rose, smiling in great relief.

"Bet you thought I wouldn't make it," said Sinbad.

"I was beginning to wonder," Proteus replied. Then he realized that something was missing. "The Book?" he asked.

"I did my best," said Sinbad quietly. "It wasn't enough."

Proteus looked at him in disbelief. "No . . . You came back anyway."

"How could I do anything else . . . my friend?"

There was a difficult moment as they both struggled with their emotions. Then Sinbad smiled wryly, turning to the block in resignation.

At the sound of Spike's cries, Sinbad hesitated. But he didn't look back. Marina held back Spike, who barked and pulled at his rope. The pain of seeing her own agony was obvious on Proteus's face.

Sinbad knelt down at the block. As the executioner raised his axe once more, Marina bent down to Spike and buried her face in his fur.

The executioner held his axe high and Sinbad closed his eyes. The axe was brought down . . . and exploded into millions of harmless metal fragments. Sinbad opened his eyes, shocked that he had been spared.

A terrifying hurricane cloud swirled over the devastated city of Syracuse. Shadows throughout the city bled and twisted into one gigantic dark form, which made its serpentine way toward the platform as Sinbad staggered to his feet.

Dymas's guards sprang forward in defense, only to fall back again as Eris appeared from the black vortex. She was gigantic and utterly terrifying in her fury, the fiery red X blazing even brighter on her chest.

"*How dare you?*" she raged at Sinbad. "Everything was going perfectly! Centuries of putting all the pieces in place and now. . . you do *this?*" As Eris's fury grew, the red X on her chest burned hotter and hotter.

"Eris? I don't understand," Sinbad stammered.

"Don't play coy with me," the goddess ranted, hovering over Sinbad like a great enraged hornet. "You're a selfish, unprincipled liar!"

Suddenly it dawned on Sinbad. "Wait a minute," he said. "I didn't lie. I came back! That's why you're here! This was all part of your test. I told the truth! And wasn't there something about being 'bound for all eternity'?"

Eris raised a fist over Sinbad, the red X on her chest blazing wildly. She struggled with the urge to crush Sinbad, but ultimately she had to relent. "Ahrg," she said in a strangled voice, swinging her clenched fist down.

As her fist approached Sinbad, it slowed. She opened her hand, and there it was: the Book of Peace.

Sinbad grabbed the Book. "Well . . . well . . . well. This has got to be a little embarrassing for you, Eris," he said.

Suddenly, she zoomed forward, her face blazing with horrifying malevolence. "Don't push your luck, Sinbad," she said in a lethal whisper. "You're cute, but not that cute." She looked hard at him. "Another time," she vowed. "Another place." Then she swirled away.

Sinbad held the Book for the first time, and a small, reverent sigh escaped his lips. It was magnificent. As the last wisps of Eris vanished, he took stock of the desecrated city: ships half sunk in parched canals; craggy, unforgiving rocks once hidden by mist; tangled, skeletal architecture looming against the wounded sky.

Syracuse was a desolate shadow of its former glory.

The crowd, once gathered to watch his execution, now stood by in stunned and aching silence as Sinbad, alone in the center of the city, opened the Book of Peace.

The light from the Book burst forth, radiating outward and illuminating the shadowed city. In the wake of the light, like so much soot and ash, every cloud, crack, stain, and fracture was blown from the city, leaving it whole again, glowing and magical, just as the gods had intended.

Sinbad, still standing on the platform, held the Book open before the gaping stares of all assembled. Proteus rushed to his side.

"For what it's worth," Proteus said to his friend, "I think the council believes you now."

"Ya think?" said Sinbad warmly.

The king approached the platform. Sinbad smiled and held the Book out to him. "King Dymas," he said.

Dymas wore a grateful smile as he reached for the Book, whereupon Sinbad playfully pulled it back. "Whoa," said Sinbad. "Hey . . . How much you got on you?"

King Dymas laughed and reached for the Book again.

"I offer you the gratitude of the Twelve Cities, and the apology of a king," said Dymas.

"No, really. How much?" Sinbad laughed as he handed the Book over to King Dymas. Dymas held the Book up for the assembled crowd.

Proteus rejoined Sinbad, looking skyward to where Eris had disappeared. "C'mon," he said. "Everyone's going to want to hear about the voyage."

Proteus started to join the crowd, but Sinbad didn't move. "Fair winds and calm seas," he said. "Nothing much to tell."

"What's the matter?" asked Proteus. "No fun if you're actually invited?"

Sinbad laughed. Looking past Proteus, he saw Rat standing with a pretty ambassador, already looking as if he'd fallen in love. Kale was talking to a dignitary who looked nervous with the enormous, earringed sailor. Sinbad knew the best place for him and his crew was at sea. They didn't belong here.

"It's just that there's a hammock in Fiji with my name on it," said Sinbad.

Sinbad shifted his gaze to Marina, and they shared a long good-bye look. Proteus could not help but see their connection.

"Good sailing, Sinbad," said Proteus.

"Get a haircut—you're going to be king someday," Sinbad joked, walking away.

Finally, Proteus moved to Marina's side. He put an arm around her, and together they walked off the platform and into the cheering crowd.

CHAPTER THIRTEEN

Later that day, Marina stood alone on a quiet balcony overlooking the beautiful palace gardens, and in the distance, the Syracuse harbor. Proteus walked out to join her. "Just another uneventful day in Syracuse," he said.

Marina turned to him, laughing softly at the understatement.

Proteus watched her looking out over the water. "You know," he said, "I stood here with a woman once. She looked over the ocean and wished she could sail beyond the horizon. She saw . . . such wonder."

"And what happened to this woman?" Marina asked him.

"She got her chance. She sailed the seas . . . and she fell in love."

Marina sighed. "Proteus, I—" she began.

He smiled. "Marina," he said, "follow your heart. Mine is here in Syracuse. Yours . . . yours is sailing with the next tide."

Marina hugged Proteus gratefully. He understood. "Oh, Proteus—thank you!" she cried.

It was now sunset. The *Chimera* sat moored in the harbor. Sinbad stood on the top deck, deep in thought, staring at the city of Syracuse, which shone and sparkled like never before. It was as if the depression that had earlier filled the black, smoking ruins of the city had given way to a joy that made Syracuse glow. Its spires and domed roofs climbed triumphantly to the golden clouds.

Spike sat listlessly at Sinbad's feet. Behind him, the crew worked quietly. Something did not feel right. Something was missing.

As the crew prepared to cast off and sail away from Syracuse, Sinbad looked around at his ship, ragged from the long journey. "You know," he mused aloud, "these joints were from the Jasmine Sea. That's halfway around the world."

"Then we'd better get started."

Surprised by the decidedly feminine voice above him, Sinbad turned, looked up at the crow's nest, and grinned. He grabbed hold of a line, and cut it. The rope swiftly pulled him up to the yardarm, where he landed gracefully and walked over to Marina in the crow's nest.

The rest of the crew had gathered on the deck, smiling at the pair.

"Well, now," said Sinbad, "that means going through the Hydra's Lair."

"Mm-hmm," she said, smiling happily.

"The Minotaur's Haven," he added.

"Mm-hmm."

"The Cyclops's Den."

"Mm-hmm."

Sinbad moved closer to Marina. "Under the Swansea Bridge . . ."

"Mm-hmm."

"Through the China Seas," Sinbad told her. "That's a very long voyage and it's . . . very, very dangerous." He was very close to her now.

"Don't worry," Marina murmured, "I'll protect you."

She threw her arms around him and they kissed as the *Chimera* sailed into the sunset.